D1572165

THIRTY
CORPSES
EVERY
thursday

THE FREDRIC BROWN PULP DETECTIVE SERIES

And, ..., more to come!

The **Fredric Brown Pulp Detective Series** presents the best of his previously uncollected work, plus some previously unpublished material, primarily in the mystery genre, but also including some sf and fantasy pieces.

THIRTY CORPSES EVERY thursday

●

**Fredric Brown
in the
Detective Pulps
VOL.6**

1986

Cover design by William L. McMillan.

FIRST PAPERBACK EDITION
Published August 1986

Dennis McMillan Publications
1995 Calais Dr. No. 3
Miami Beach, FL 33141

CONTENTS

INTRODUCTION

Bill Nolan seems to have covered Fred Brown's later history well; the following are my earlier memories of that innovative man.

We had a writer's group in Milwaukee which is still in existence, The Allied Authors. We were all new to the trade with a few five dollar sales to newspaper syndicates who published short-short stories. Fred joined soon after it was organized in the early 1930's.

Bob Bloch also had a group in Milwaukee but they were closer to professionalism than we were. Larry Sternig, now an agent and still working out of Milwaukee, was our ace market hunter. He was the one who discovered some magazines in Philadelphia which published what they considered sex stories. I think the dirtiest word we used was "curvaceous." They bought longer stories than the syndicates and paid the exorbitant price of one third of a cent a word for them.

The publisher was called Shade Publications; the two magazines we settled on were titled *Paris Nights* and *Scarlet Adventuress*. I used the name Roney Scott for them; I forget what the others used. Robert Leslie Bellem was their big man and he used his own name. We had higher goals in sight.

It was through our sales there that Fred and I finally got an agent to handle us. His name was (and is) Harry Altshuler but he wrote his stories for Shade under (I think) Frederick Faust. He was a student at Temple University. When we had trouble getting our money out of Shade, Harry suggested that he be our agent and collect the money.

Decades later, we both left Harry. The trouble with Harry, we felt, was that he was a fine and decent man. They make bad agents. In our house one night when Dave Dresser was here (Santa Barbara) Fred mentioned his discontent and Dresser (Brett Halliday) suggested he try Scott Meredith. So that's where Fred wound up. I wound up on higher ground with the Harold Matson Company. Fred should have waited.

But back to Milwaukee. It was Fred who suggested, when the mystery magazines were on the wane, that I try some science fiction magazines, which were doing a lot better. Judging by their conference attendance, I do believe that science fiction fans are much more numerous than mystery fans.

So I wrote a couple, and they sold. Then Tony Boucher, who was runing *Fantasy and Science Fiction Magazine* (I think) wrote to me and asked for a story. I sent him one called "Horse's Asteroid." He would publish it, he told me, but not under that title. He went on to explain that, as a writer, he had written one called "A Kiss for Uranus," and that had also needed a title change.

In toto, I wrote thirteen s-f stories and sold eleven of them. But they were not my natural field. Most s-f readers will agree. But Fred took me through a transition period; thank you, Fred, wherever you are.

Back to Milwaukee: Leo Margulies, an editor at Thrilling Publications, was a fervent Brown fan. After Fred's first book came out he still wasn't making enough money to quit his job as proofreader at the *Milwaukee Journal,* where he was making (in those cheaper days) over a hundred dollars a week. But Margulies told him he would pay him "seventy-five" and Fred assumed that meant seventy-five hundred dollars a year. So off to New York Fred went.

Two weeks later he learned it meant seventy-five dollars a week. Fred quit. From now on, he decided, he would be a full time professional writer.

He was that and more. He had, I think, the most innovative mind in the science fiction field, dwelling on the characters, not the mechanics. He probably didn't have Bradbury's lyricism but he certainly had a better brain and more acceptable characterization. But I speak from ignorance; I am not an s-f fan.

When Fred was working at Cuneo Press in Milwaukee as a proofreader, I used to pick him up after work (he didn't have a car) and take him out to a local short, nine hole golf course. We played for small stakes and Fred was slightly more inept than I was, so I usually picked up fifteen or twenty cents. The last time we played, Fred missed a two-foot putt on the last hole that cost him a nickel. He glared at the ball, looked at me, twisted his putter into a loop, and said, "That is the last round of golf I will ever play." It was. I should have followed his example.

Fred's first book, as Nolan said, was rejected often before it was accepted by Dutton and received an Edgar award as the best "first" mystery of the year. In those days, they didn't give out a best mystery award, avoiding petulance among the successful pros.

My first was turned down by Gold Medal, then offered to Dutton. Fred, who was living in New York at the time, sat in the Dutton office when the book was being considered and assured them that if they bought it it would win a first novel Edgar. They did and it did. Thank you for that, too, dead friend.

Where do we go from here? It was a better time, those days, depression and war notwithstanding. We wrote and they bought. We wrote fast; they bought cheaply. But they bought. They didn't assume it would make them rich; all they asked for was reasonable returns and reader interest.

Today, with Waldenbooks and B. Dalton running the show, you will need an impressive history of big sales even to be considered by them. It would be comfortable to think that the garbage that leads the best seller lists is a new trend in America. It isn't. Check your old *World Almanac*s to confirm that. The best sellers of those years are no longer being reprinted; many pulp writers are. Do we have to die to be appreciated?

It doesn't matter. We are doing what we want to do and getting paid for it. There is no higher reward than that.

William Campbell Gault
Santa Barbara, California
February 1985

MURDER DRAWS A crowd

At the corner of Fourteenth and Rusk, the shabby-looking man in the shell-rimmed glasses stopped and looked around him, then leaned against a telephone pole to wait.

The next man to arrive looked like a broker. Then a stenographer with a folded newspaper under her arm. Then others.

They glanced from time to time at the clock in the Herald-News Building across the street. It was still seventeen minutes before two o'clock.

A few glanced casually at the blind man a few paces from the corner, seated on the hard sidewalk with his back against the building behind him. One man dropped a nickel into the tin cup, then turned away to look at the clock again.

At five minutes before two they began to arrive in droves. The corner was jammed, and a few people were forced off the curb.

Someone chanced to look out the editorial room of the *Herald-News*, called out to someone else, and a dozen heads popped out of windows to look at the crowd across the street.

Back behind another window a photographer's flash bulb flared, and through that window the crowd saw the stubby nose of a camera.

A copy boy strolled into the editorial room and grinned at the city editor.

"I just asked one of 'em," he said. "There was an item in the *Tribune*,. . . Movietone's going to make a crowd scene at two o'clock and anybody wants their mug in the movies could be there. Did the *Tribune* scoop us?"

The city editor growled. He motioned to Bates, his star leg-man, and glowered as Bates approached his desk.

The reporter beat him to the gun. "Say, Harry, is everyone on the wanted desk nuts?" he demanded. "Running an ad that any fool could see meant a story, and not tipping us off?"

"What ad, Bates?"

"The ad for a hundred men and women to show up across the street at two o'clock for a few hours work distributing campaign literature at ten bucks apiece. It's a gag. Why should anyone pay ten bucks for something like that?"

The city editor's eyes opened wide, and he sat up straighter. "Get the hell out there and find out what it's about. The Trib said Movietone wanted a mob scene there. Something's up. G'wan and get the story."

The reporter ran for the elevator. As he was running out of the door to the street, he saw Sergeant Garvan. The sergeant was looking at the crowd in bewilderment.

"What's up, Sarge?" the reporter asked.

"Don't know whether to move them on or not." Garvan took off his derby and scratched his bald head vigorously. "They're blocking traffic. But one of them told me the *Sentinel* ran an ad for WLAR offering twenty smackers to anyone who got in on their special Man-On-The-Street broadcast at two. But it's time now, and where's the sound truck?"

The reporter's eyes widened. "Come on over there with me, Sarge. Something's awful rotten in the state of,. . ."

In the heart of the crowd across the street, a woman screamed.

It was a scream of sheer horror. Before it died away, Garvan and Bates were across the street, fighting their way into the jam.

When Roger B. Langtry, proprietor of the Langtry Detective Agency, better known as Deadpan Langtry, swung down from the New York Limited and strode through the station, he was worried.

True, he had just finished a satisfactory bit of work, but the trail had taken him out of town at a most unfortunate moment.

Five minutes before he had to leave the office, a call had come in from J.D. Burchard, asking that he or a representative call at once to accept a case. And a case from a big banker like J.D. Burchard, Langtry knew, was important business.

He'd had to send Bill Ford, and he was wondering how Bill had made out with the case. Bill was better with his legs than his head. Maybe, too, Bill read too many detective stories or something.

Anyway, he always tried to do things the spectacular way instead of the sensible way.

If he could only have stayed in town long enough to hear Burchard's story and to get Bill started off on the right foot, he'd feel a lot better about it. And a lot could have happened in four days.

Anyhow, he was glad to be back. He set off briskly to walk the six blocks from the depot to his office.

It was just as Deadpan Langtry turned into Rusk Avenue off Thirteenth and saw the crowd on the corner a block away, that the woman screamed.

He saw Sergeant Garvan and the reporter, both of whom he recognized, running across the street. By the time they got there, he was halfway down the block, running.

Women didn't scream like *that*, he knew, when someone stepped on their toes in a crowd.

He plunged ruthlessly into the mob. Those on the inside were pushing back and those on the outside pressing forward to find out what had happened.

Langtry reached the focus of attention at almost the same time Garvan and the reporter got there. It was the blind begger. He still sat with his back leaning against the building behind him, but his head had fallen forward. His hands dropped limply, tin cup and pencils fallen from their grasp.

And the front of his shirt was wet and unpleasantly red.

Sergeant Garvan put a hand on the blind man's forehead, tilted his head upright. His throat had been neatly slit. His glasses fell off; Garvan noticed that they were dark, but not opaque, glass.

"Been dead five or ten minutes," he said. "Somebody did a good job of it."

"Know him, Sarge?" asked the reporter.

Garvan shook his head. He looked again at the transparent dark glasses, then lifted one closed eyelid of the dead man with an exploring thumb. "His eyes look to me like they were all right."

"They *were* all right," said Deadpan, looking over his shoulder.

Garvan whirled, surprised to find the private detective behind him. "Mean you know who he is?"

Langtry nodded. "My best operative, Bill Ford."

When the homicide squad arrived, Deadpan went with the sergeant to the chief's office. The chief was hard to convince.

"You're trying to tell me, Langtry," he demanded, "that you don't even know who your own operative was working for?"

"That's right," lied Deadpan. "I tell you I was out of town for four days. You can check that. Ford wasn't doing a thing when I left. Maybe someone offered a case and he started work while waiting for me to get back."

"Did he have authority to do that?"

The private detective shrugged. "Not exactly, but he might have."

The chief glared at him, trying to judge how much or how little he knew, and gave it up as a hopeless job.

Deadpan Langtry was well nicknamed. Once he had had the fortune and misfortune to capture a peterman who was full of coke to the eyebrows and who had a bottle of nitro-glycerine in his pocket.

The cops had completed the arrest with the aid of blotting paper, and after a month in a hospital under the care of a plastic surgeon, Langtry had emerged with a rugged but synthetic face, a face whose muscles thenceforward failed to co-ordinate with his emotions. It was a face made to order for a poker player, . . . or a private detective.

The chief turned to Garvan. "Go round to Langtry's office with him and question his stenographer. Ford may have told her something, or may have turned in reports. Then *stick with this guy.* Let him investigate in his own sweet way, but stay with him."

They took a cab to Langtry's office. June Smith, his secretary, looked up and smiled as they entered.

"What was Bill Ford working on, June?" asked Deadpan. His right hand reached for the pencil in his vest pocket, touched it. She caught the signal.

"I haven't an idea. He was hanging around here until yesterday noon. I haven't seen him since. Have a good trip?"

Deadpan knew she'd find out soon enough about Bill Ford, so he didn't stall. "June, Bill is dead," he said softly. "Someone killed him an hour ago."

The girl turned slightly pale, but didn't say anything.

Langtry went on: "If anyone offers a case, no dice until this is settled. And there's something you can do. Get copies of all papers for the four days I've been away and study them, every item, every ad. Later report anything unusual you find."

When they reached the lobby of the building, Garvan demanded, "What you expect her to find in the papers? We already know about the screwy want-ads and the fake news item the killer used to draw the crowd."

"She won't find anything else. But I didn't want her to get hysterical. I gave her something to do to keep her mind occupied; it'll make it easier to ease through the first shock. She liked Bill a lot."

Garvan grunted. "Where you starting?"

"The *Herald-News*. I want a look at that photo someone was smart enough to snap out the window."

The photographer turned out to be tall and redheaded and he wore shell-rimmed glasses. He told them his name was Willis.

"Here's a copy of the print," he said, handing one to Langtry. "It's running four columns on the front page of the final, but this glossy print shows up clearer than a stereotype, naturally."

"With direct sun on the crowd," asked Deadpan, "how come you used the flash-bulb? It couldn't have done much good at that distance."

"The flash-bulb," Willis explained, "was timed a second before the shutter. They weren't synchronized. The flash made the crowd look this way, and gave me full front views of almost everyone. It's an old gag, but good."

Deadpan nodded. "How'd you happen to spot the crowd and take the picture?"

"I got an anonymous call. A guy with a phony lisp and a disguised voice phoned here a bit before two and told me to shoot out the window at two if I wanted a good pic. I shot from the darkroom window; it's got a trick light-tight shade, of course, but it can be raised, and the angle was better from there. It was a timed shot; I set the shutter for two o'clock on the head."

"Why not just snap it?"

"I didn't know what was coming off. When I got that call I looked out, of course, and saw the crowd, but that mightn't mean anything. The call might have meant something special was coming off at two, and if so I wanted that in the shot, naturally."

"The anonymous call, . . . any way of tracing it?"

The photographer shook his head. "We tried. Girl at the want-ad desk remembers the call we got on the want-ad, but the switchboard girl doesn't remember anything about the other call. She takes a dozen a minute."

Langtry studied the photograph Willis had given him. It was an excellent shot, in perfect focus, almost every face recognizable.

Garvan looked at it over his shoulder. "But why," he demanded, "should the killer have wanted this taken? Maybe his own mug is on there. The homicide boys are probably working that angle now."

Deadpan handed him the picture. "They'll waste their time. The killer knew a shot was going to be snapped at two, so the killer wouldn't be in that picture. But maybe Bill Ford was being killed just when this was being snapped."

Sergeant Garvan took off his derby and scratched his head thoughtfully. "You mean," he said slowly, "maybe the killer figured that when the picture was taken the crowd would look that way and choose that minute to lean over with his knife or razor?"

The private detective nodded. "He couldn't have been sure of the *exact* time of the shot, so in the crowd he'd never have faced this way at all. He worked his way near Bill, and when it got near two, he would have stooped over like he was talking to him, and maybe he was, and then 'flash!' and everybody but him looks this way. And that's his chance."

Garvan nodded slowly. "Yeah. And in a crowd that thick, nobody'd notice him anyway. And if he'd stooped down over the blind man—I mean over Bill Ford—nobody'd have noticed. But where does that get us?"

"Nowhere yet," said Langtry. "We'll talk to that girl on the want-ad desk." He turned back to the photographer. "By the way, Willis, how come you used a timer? You could have snapped it at two o'clock without one, couldn't you?"

"That shot wasn't the only one. The call came in a few minutes before two, but I had time to rig the camera in the darkroom. Then I took my candid into the empty office across the hall and took a shot or two from there. When the flash went off I came back and developed all the films. The candid shots weren't as good as the other. I didn't enlarge them."

He handed Langtry two small prints, and the private detective handed one to the sergeant and examined the other closely himself.

"Golly," said Garvan, "These may be more important than the other. The killer couldn't have known these were being taken. He wouldn't have figured on snaps from this angle."

Langtry nodded soberly. "We'll study these later under a magnifying glass. Offhand, they don't seem to show anything in particular. Come on, let's see the want-ad girl, Sarge. Thanks, Willis."

One of the girls at the want-ad desk was slightly red around the eyes, and when they came near, her glance took in Garvan's derby and square-toed shoes. She sighed wearily.

"Can't you let me alone," she wanted to know plaintively. "I've told about it ten times to the bosses here, and the city editor, and the chief of police, and more detectives and reporters, and now *you* come."

Deadpan took a ten-spot from his pocket and tucked it under her pad of paper. "Go buy yourself ice cream sodas and drown your sorrows when you get off work. I'm not a cop, but the man who was killed worked for me. My name is Langtry."

The girl's resentment dropped from her. Maybe it was the ten-spot, maybe the approach. Probably both.

"The call came in late, just as we were closing the early edition. Whoever called said he was calling for Harry Ganz, and he dictated the ad just as it ran. Said we had to get it in the first edition."

"You don't take want-ads without advance payment from strangers, do you?" Langtry asked.

"No, but how was I to know it was phony? Harry Ganz isn't only a big politician, but he owns stock in the paper. And there wasn't time to investigate. I sent it right to the composing room with a 'must' stamp. They got it in, and nobody thought anything about it until afterward."

"The voice on the phone?" Deadpan leaned forward to listen carefully.

"A man's. High-pitched. Thinking back, I guess it was disguised all right. And he lisped—'ten dollarth for dithtributing, . . .' "

"Okay, kid," said Deadpan, turning away. "Don't get too tight on all those ice cream sodas tonight."

He stopped just outside the door in the hallway, and Garvan bumped into him. "Where next, Langtry?" he asked. "Gonna check on the other news and ad items? The radio ad in the *Sentinel* and the Movietone item in the *Tribune*?"

The private detective shook his head thoughtfully. "No use. If there is any information there, the homicide boys will get it. But all they'll find out is that in each case the dope came in just before deadline, from a guy with a disguised voice and a lisp. We won't waste time on it."

He started walking again, reached the elevator door just as it opened. Langtry pushed Garvan inside, stepped aside courteously to let a fat woman get in ahead of him. Then he turned and sprinted back down the hall as the door clanged shut.

He opened the door and went back into the photographer's office. The darkroom door opened and Willis stuck his head out.

"Mind if I use your phone a minute?" Deadpan asked. He was already reaching for it. The photographer nodded cheerfully.

"Get me Delaware 4224, quick," he barked into the phone. "Perry National Bank? Give me your vice-president, J.D. Burchard, quickly,... Hello, Mr. Burchard? This is Langtry. Heard the news? I just got back in town,... Yes, I'll keep your name out of it, if I possibly can. Shall I see you at the bank, or at home?...Okay, then, at eight o'clock."

He replaced the receiver and strolled back into the hallway. Garvan came pounding down the stairs, looking for him.

"Hi, Sarge," he called out. "That was an up car. Didn't you notice? Anyway, it's only one flight to the street. Let's walk down."

Garvan looked at him suspiciously, then fell into stride alongside as they went down the stairway to the street.

"Got your roller skates, Sarge?" he asked. "We're going places."

"Where?" demanded Garvan, as they walked rapidly west on Fourteenth Street.

Langtry didn't answer. One reason was that he didn't know. Before he saw Burchard at eight, he wanted to walk and to think, to let the few facts he knew digest themselves, fall into place in the picture.

He walked rapidly but aimlessly. Several miles later they found themselves back almost at their starting point. Garvan was beginning to puff.

"Listen, Langtry," he complained. "If you're going in circles, let's take a cab. We'll get there faster."

Deadpan looked at his wrist watch and saw that he'd have to get rid of Garvan soon if he wanted to keep his appointment with Burchard.

He started walking again, more rapidly than before, and this time in a straight line for the outskirts of the city. Seven-thirty found them in quiet streets where there wasn't any traffic. The private detective stopped on a corner and Garvan caught up with him, looking as though he had been run through a wringer.

"Don't you ever eat?" he complained.

Deadpan ignored the question. "Got your gun on you?" he asked. The sergeant shook his head.

"How's your wind?"

Garvan mopped his brow and found breath to answer, "My what?"

Langtry turned and began to sprint. "Come on, Sarge," he called back over his shoulder. "Stick with me."

A block farther on he glanced back again. The sergeant had given up and was sitting on the curbstone talking to himself.

Langtry ran on. Three blocks later he came to an arterial and managed to flag a cab. He gave the driver the home address of Burchard, and glanced again at his wrist watch. It was ten minutes before eight.

At Burchard's home, a servant admitted him. "Mr. Burchard expects you," he said when he had heard Langtry's name. "He's in his study, second door on the left."

"Okay." Deadpan strode past him and went on back to the study. The door was an inch ajar and he knocked and opened it in the same movement. Then he stood staring into the room.

Slumped back in his chair was the body of Burchard, with a bullet hole through his chest and a broad red stain around it. Quickly he crossed the room toward the banker, looking for some sign of life, but there wasn't any. The body was cold; Burchard had been dead for some time. Over half an hour, Langtry decided.

He wasted no time blaming himself. It had been while he was in the taxi that a sudden hunch had come to him, that the pieces of the mystery had begun to fall into place in his mind. And Burchard was dead by then; it would have been too late to save him.

He looked around quickly but carefully. There was nothing to help him. There was an open window through which the shot could have come. Papers from the desk were scattered about, and the desk drawers were open. That was all.

He saw a button on the side of the desk which would probably bring a servant, and he reached for it, then hesitated. There was something he could do before he sent for the police.

He grabbed a phone book, looked up a name, address, and phone number and wrote them down. Then he dialed the number.

Willis, the *Herald-News* photographer, answered.

Deadpan explained; "I'm still working on why the killer wanted that photo taken. About these candid shots, . . . what time were they snapped?"

"Shortly before two o'clock. I didn't notice exactly."

"And the call, Willis. Do you remember exactly what the guy said?"

"Perfectly. I can remember the exact wording. He said: 'You're a *Herald* photographer? If you want a good picture, look out of your window at two o'clock.' Then he hung up on me."

"Thanks," said Deadpan. "You can't remember anything else that might help?"

"Not a thing. That's every word he said."

The private detective hung up and then dialed June's number, waited impatiently until she answered.

"Listen, June. I ducked Sergeant Garvan. He's been trailing me all day. He'll probably try to locate me through you. If he does, tell him to hurry to the corner of Twenty-eighth and Burleigh and wait for me. I may need him this time."

He stemmed June's eager torrent of questions. "Yeah, the case is cracked. If Garvan doesn't come around soon, leave word at headquarters to have him phone you. He's sure to call in there. And listen: I couldn't ask you today. Had Bill Ford told you anything at all about what he was doing for Burchard?"

"Not much, Chief. Burchard was being blackmailed. Something about him and a woman. It wasn't the woman who was blackmailing him; he didn't know who it was. But he had a lead, and Bill was following that lead to get the identity of the blackmailer."

"Okay, June. That fits in. Get some sleep."

He replaced the phone and rang for the servant. He'd worked

fast; it had been less than five minutes since he'd been admitted at the door.

The servant stopped in the doorway, turned pale.

"Your employer has been killed," the private detective told him calmly. "You'd better phone the police. I'm going on; I can't wait till they get here." Then as he read correctly the horrified expression on the man's face. "No, I didn't do it. Look and you'll see he's been dead almost an hour."

As the man started toward the telephone, Deadpan brushed by him and strode out into the night again. At a busy corner nearby, he hailed a cruising cab and directed it to Twenty-eighth and Burleigh.

When the cab left him on the corner, his interest centered on a small two-story house three doors from the corner. There was a light on the second floor.

On the corner itself stood a four-story apartment building. Deadpan entered it, climbed to the fourth floor, and found what he had hoped to find—a window opening off the fourth floor hallway which gave him a bird's eye view of the neighborhood, and of the house which interested him.

His eyes lit up when he saw that there was a skylight in the roof of that house—a skylight over a lighted room. From the apartment building window he could see only a picture on one wall of the room with the skylight.

He retraced his steps down the four flights of stairs and out to the sidewalk. Looking carefully about to be sure he wasn't observed, he crossed the grass and walked around behind the two-story house to the back porch which he had also noticed from the apartment building window.

Silently he climbed to the porch railing and shinned up a post. He caught the edge of the roof with strong hands and drew himself up. From there it was easy to climb to the roof proper, and an instant later he knelt beside the skylight.

He looked down into a photographer's studio. Willis, the tall redheaded photographer of the *Herald-News*, was working at a table. Equipment was lined neatly around the walls.

On the table beside Willis lay a revolver with a silencer. Now Deadpan was certain beyond doubt that his hunch was correct. And the silencer explained why Burchard's servants had not heard a shot.

As he looked down, Langtry ran over in his mind the points that had led him to Willis. He believed that they were sufficient, that with evidence he could find in the studio and with the aid of ballistics to link that silenced revolver with the bullet in the body of the banker, he could prove his case. Soon he'd go down and wait for Sergeant Garvan on the corner, and tell him to make the arrest. Maybe Garvan was already there.

Some of the motivation was still obscure, but it could be guessed at. Bill Ford had obviously been checking the comings and goings of a *Herald-News* employee. The lead to the identity of Burchard's anonymous blackmailer, which Burchard had given Ford at that first interview, was carrying Ford in the right direction.

And Willis had spotted Ford. Possibly he'd seen Ford trailing him, and then had recognized him as the blind beggar who'd taken up a stand across the street from the *Herald-News*. Willis would be watching for things like that. And his plans had been made carefully to eliminate Bill Ford.

He'd had ample opportunity, after he'd made arrangements to collect the crowd that would shield his movements. He'd set the timer on his camera at about, Deadpan estimated, five minutes to two, leaving the camera in the darkroom where it wouldn't be noticed by other employees.

Then he had hurriedly snapped a couple of candid shots of the crowd, run down one flight of stairs to the street and had been standing in front of Bill when the flash bulb had warned him that the camera was about to click, and had made all others in the crowd look toward it. Then he'd leaned down, taken a slash with a knife or razor, and returned, had been starting to develop his shots when the crime was discovered.

Now Willis was working with some prints. Langtry leaned forward to try to make out what they were, and rested his weight on a cross-brace of the skylight. There was a sudden crash of glass as the skylight gave way under him.

He didn't lose consciousness, although for the first moment he was a bit dazed. He was lying on the floor of the studio, one arm crumpled uselessly under him, blood streaming from cuts in his face.

And Willis, over the muzzle of the gun with the silencer, was looking at him grimly.

The private detective shook his head to clear it. If he could get Willis to talk, maybe he could think of some way out. "Don't put another killing on the books," he said. "The place is surrounded."

"Nuts," said the photographer. "You came here alone spying, or you'd have brought the coppers up. What led you here?" Willis' finger didn't relax on the trigger, but there was some curiosity in his voice.

"If it wasn't you," said Deadpan, "how'd the killer have known you'd shoot that flash-bulb before the photo, to warn him to duck? And you heard me phone Burchard and arrange to see him at eight. That's how you beat me to him. You knew whatever lead he'd given Ford would have led me to you too."

Willis grunted. He raised the revolver to take aim.

Deadpan tried again: "You don't want to shoot me. It would mean you'd have to blow town. You'd have to leave behind the nice blackmail racket you've built up. As a newspaper photographer you've probably had lots of opportunities. It'd mean you'd be wanted. You wouldn't dare try to work as a photographer anywhere else."

The thrust had hit home hard enough to delay the bullet from that silenced gun another minute.

"What's the out?" Willis demanded. "What happens if I don't kill you and blow? Even if you can't prove your charges, I'm sunk. My prints are on record in Chi, and it isn't for reckless driving. If I'm booked on this, I'm done, even if you can't prove it."

Deadpan saw now why Willis hadn't hesitated to commit murder when he found he was being trailed. If he was booked for blackmail, his Chicago crime would come out and he'd get the chair; he had nothing to lose by another killing.

Deadpan saw the muzzle coming up. "You've got one out without having to kill me. One that would let you get away from everything you've done so far."

Deadpan had managed to raise himself on his good elbow. He knew it was now or never. Willis was thinking his last remark over. In a minute he'd ask, "Well, what's the out?" and Langtry didn't know. He'd just been stalling.

It was a long shot, but he'd used it once before. He swung his legs toward Willis'; his left foot hooked behind the photographer's ankle and his right heel crashed hard against the killer's kneecap.

As he moved, the silenced revolver spat viciously. Deadpan felt a sensation as though a branding iron had been drawn against the side of his neck. Then the revolver clattered against the floor as Willis went down with a shattered kneecap. Langtry twisted around, got to the revolver first.

He struggled to his feet and staggered to the window fronting on the street. He couldn't see as far as the corner to see whether Garvan was there yet, but he took a camera from a stand and hurled it through the glass to the sidewalk.

The sergeant came running, looking upward to the broken window. Deadpan motioned to him.

Willis was dragging himself across the floor toward an open doorway that the detective could see led to a bathroom. Deadpan let him go, ran to the table and gathered up the prints the photographer had been sorting. He found more in the drawer of the table.

He could hear the sergeant pounding at the outer door, trying to break it down. Deadpan wasn't in any hurry now about the sergeant. The prints were what interested him. He found the one that had obviously been the basis of the blackmail of Burchard. And there were others, similar, which showed Willis had a lucrative sideline.

He piled the prints on the table and struck a match. Just as he ignited the pile, he heard the outer door give way under Garvan's battering.

The bathroom door clicked from the inside as Garvan burst into the room. He looked at Langtry, who had fallen back limply into a chair, took in his cut and bleeding face, the broken skylight, and the flaming pile of prints and negatives on the table.

Deadpan pointed to the bathroom door. "He's in there. Go ahead and bust in. He's had time."

"Time to what?" The sergeant tried the knob, then threw his shoulder against the door. It crashed open on his second lunge and he went headlong into the bathroom. He came out looking a bit shaken.

"He got to a razor and cut himself a piece of throat. Why didn't you stop him?"

"Why should I?" the private detective asked bitterly. "That razor's probably what he killed Bill Ford with. Go ahead and phone homicide. While they're coming, I'll tell you what happened. Tell 'em to bring an ambulance, too. I got to get my wing fixed."

He finished his story just as the police cars drove up. Garvan waved to them from the window, then turned back to Langtry.

"I get most of it," he said. "But it still sounds like guesswork. You say your phone call to Willis made you sure he was guilty. How come?"

"I asked him what the message he got over the phone was, and he said the guy said, '*You're a* Herald *photographer? If you want a good picture, look out of your window at two o'clock.*' He said that was every word the guy said before he hung up. Now don't you get it?"

Garvan looked at him blankly. "Hell, no. What's wrong with that?"

Deadpan leaned forward and blew the ashes from the table before he answered. Heavy footsteps were pounding up the stairs. "Willis was the first one to mention the lisp in the disguised voice," he told the sergeant. "There aren't any s's in that spiel. Let's hear you try to lisp it."

I'LL SEE YOU AT midnight

I was sitting in Joe's hash house eating fried eggs that would have been ham-and, except that I couldn't afford the ham. I was looking at nothing more interesting than the fly specks on the back of the menu card stuck between the sugar bowl and the vinegar cruet. I was wondering nothing less interesting than where my next meal was coming from.

I hadn't noticed the tall, thin guy with the fancy clothes until he came over and dropped into the chair across the table from me. I looked at him a bit curiously, then, because he didn't look like a man who'd eat in a place like Joe's.

His suit was expensive-looking; his silk shirt had cost close to ten bucks, and there was a two-carat diamond pin in his five-dollar cravat. The get-up didn't make sense in an eaterie where the top price is thirty-five cents, and where my fried eggs cost fifteen cents, with bread and coffee for free.

The stranger caught my eye as I looked at him, and he said, "You're Larry Bonnert, aren't you?"

I nodded, and then before he could say anything else Joe was standing there looking down at him. Joe asked, "What's yours?" and from the tone of his voice I could tell that he, too, wondered how he had rated this particular customer.

"Coffee," said the tall man.

"Doughnuts or rolls?"

"Neither. Just coffee."

"They come with it," said Joe flatly. "Coffee's a nickel and you get the sinkers or sweet rolls with it. Which you want?"

The man said, "Neither. Just the coffee."

Joe walked back over to the counter and I said, "Am I supposed to know who you are?"

He shook his head and said, "You don't know me." Then he smiled faintly and took something green about the size of a calling card from his pocket and put it on the table in front of me. It was a dollar bill, folded twice. A new bill.

I picked it up and turned it over to be sure, and it wasn't a dollar; it was a fifty. A fifty-dollar bill; I'd fogotten that such things existed.

I said, "What for?"

Then Joe was coming back, and I put the bill hastily into my pocket so Joe wouldn't notice. Joe brought a mug of coffee in one hand and a plate with two sweet rolls in the other. He put the coffee down in front of the man across from me, and the sweet rolls beside my plate. He said, not exactly to either of us, "They're paid for. Somebody might as well eat them."

I said, "Thanks, Joe."

The stranger had taken a handful of change out of his vest pocket and was sorting through it. There wasn't anything there smaller than a quarter. He handed Joe a quarter and said, "Keep the change."

Joe looked at the quarter in his hand as though it was a snail or a frog or something, then walked away.

I said, "I stuck that bill in my pocket to get it out of sight. That doesn't mean I'm taking it, yet. I want to know what for."

He said, "That's for nothing. Or, let's say, that's for listening. To what I'm going to say."

I said, "What—" and then stopped because Joe was coming back. He put down two dimes in front of the man across from me and then walked back to the counter.

I glanced at the dimes. "Better put them in your pocket. If you walk out and leave them there, Joe'll follow you outside and make you eat them. You rubbed him the wrong way. And you're rubbing me the wrong way, too."

He said, "I'm paying for the privilege."

"I haven't taken it yet. Go on and talk. When you're through, maybe I'll keep this fifty. Maybe I'll make you eat it, and the two dimes for desert."

He smiled faintly. He said, "Take it or leave it, now. It's for listening, without interrupting or getting ideas, until I've said *all* I'm going to say. Ten minutes, maybe."

There didn't seem to be any hitch to that. Fifty dollars for ten minutes isn't hay, if you get it just for listening. But there was something I didn't like about his face and something I didn't like about the way he talked.

But fifty bucks is fifty bucks. For listening.

I said, "And after the ten minutes?"

He shrugged. "It's your fifty. And it's your party; do anything you damn please."

I said, "Start talking."

He moved the mug of coffee to one side and leaned both elbows on the table. He said, "First, take a look out the window right behind you."

I turned slowly. Don't ask me how I knew, somehow, what I was going to see. Or why something tightened in my throat. Because what I saw didn't mean anything to me now.

There was a sedan parked at the curb. There was a man in the front seat, behind the wheel. A man and a girl were in the back seat, the girl on the side of the car nearest to me. Her eyes were closed and her face expressionless. She might have been asleep, sitting up, or she might have been drugged.

The girl was Geraldine.

The driver of the car must have been watching me, waiting for me to turn and look out the window, for even while I was turning my head he was swinging the car out from the curb, getting off to a fast start. In less time than it would have taken me to reach the door of Joe's, the car was around the corner out of sight.

There wasn't any way I could have chased it. Even had I run out and commandeered the first car going by, the sedan would have been hopelessly lost in the busy traffic of Calhoun Street before I could have turned the corner after it.

So I didn't try. Instead, I turned slowly back from the window to face the man sitting across from me. I saw him through what seemed to be a red haze. My hands ached in every muscle with the effort necessary to keep them off his throat.

I don't know why, because Geraldine meant less than nothing to me now. For a year I'd hated her.

But, just the same, the voice that said again, "Start talking," didn't sound like mine.

He said, "A year ago—"

A year ago things had been a lot different than they were now. I'd just got my promotion to detective sergeant, first class. I'd cracked some tough cases and I was beginning to get my name in the newspapers.

I was a tough cop, but an honest cop. And a happily married guy. Married to a girl named Geraldine. We lived in a nice little apartment and we were saving up to—But I'll skip the sob stuff, and get to what happened.

I was working on Dixie Wilman then. Dixie Wilman, the kingpin of pinball. And I had him where I wanted him, under indictment for murder, the murder of a tavernkeeper who chiseled Dixie's cut on the rolling marbles. Dixie meant it as a gentle warning to the others; I turned it into a not-so-gentle warning to Dixie. I'd been following him that night, and I was the witness who put him on the scene of the murder at the time of the murder and made it an air-tight case.

There wasn't any way out of it for Dixie, even if I were killed. I saw to that; I saw that there were sworn statements of my testimony on file where he couldn't get at them, even if he got at me.

Then, two nights before the trial, I found a note instead of Geraldine, when I went home. A note that told me whom to talk to if I ever wanted to see her again. I talked to him.

I hadn't thought of them pulling one like that, because I'd let it be known that my testimony was down on paper. But Dixie Wilman out-thought me on that one. The testimony stayed on paper, but at the trial I balled it up.

The defense lawyer tripped me up on cross-examination, punched wider and wider holes in my story that put Dixie on the scene of the crime. Finally, he trapped me into admitting perjury in order to further my career at Dixie's expense. The case was dismissed.

I was fired off the force in disgrace, and narrowly avoided standing trial myself. Only thing saved me from that was a general feeling that Dixie was probably guilty anyway, even if—without my testimony—it couldn't be proved on him.

There was another letter waiting for me when I got home that night. Geraldine was free all right, but she'd left me flat. She was going to her parents.

It knocked me off my feet, but I thought maybe she didn't know the score, why I had let a lawyer trap me that way. I wrote and explained everything.

Her answer came from Reno. A while later, the decree.

I said, "The hell with a year ago. I know more than you do about that."

The man across the table from me said, "Do you?"

The muscles in my fingers were still taut. My voice still didn't sound like my own. I don't know why; I hated Geraldine for what she'd done. But—

He said, "Dixie Wilman hated you, Bonnert. He double-crossed you. I got the inside story from one of the boys. *Your wife was never kidnaped.* They played you for a sucker."

I sat there looking at him. It didn't make sense, what he was saying.

He went on: "There was a guy named Regan. Lived in the apartment next to yours. He was out of work then. Remember him?"

I nodded. I said, "He's running a cigar store now. Down on Third Street. A nifty place."

"It ought to be. He got five thousand for his end of it. Dixie bought him."

"I don't—"

He said, "They were *going* to kidnap your wife. That was the set-up. Two days before the trial she got a message that her mother was very sick. She wrote a hurried note for you and took the first train. Begin to see it, pal? When Dixie's boys went to get her they found the note instead. Somebody was smart; they took her note and left one of theirs saying—well, you know what that note was."

The man across the table grinned at me. He went on: "There were letters from her, during the trial. Regan watched your mail box and, of course, you never got them. And didn't write. All she heard of or from you was what got in the newspapers after that fourth day of the trial, when—"

It felt like there was something stuck in my throat. I had to clear it twice before any words could come out. My mind was going in dizzying circles. It still didn't make sense all the way, and I grabbed at one thing that didn't. I said, "But the day—that day I got home after I'd done what Dixie wanted in court, that note that she was free but was leaving—"

He said, "They had several of her letters to you that Regan had intercepted. A good penman wrote that note. It said she was leaving you and going to her parents' place. You wrote her and explained. I can guess what was in that letter you wrote, from what happened."

I said, "It *did* explain."

"Did it?" he asked.

Sure, it had—*or had it,* on the assumption that she'd never been kidnaped and didn't know what I was talking about when I said I'd perjured myself for her sake and that she—

Weren't there two ways she could take that, and both wrong? That I'd lied in the first place about trailing Wilman to the scene of the murder, in order to advance my career by pinning a rap on him. Or that I'd told the truth then, and had accepted bribery "for her sake" to discredit that testimony at the trial. In either case, branding myself as a crook—or what is worse, a crooked detective.

And that, sandwiched in with angry recriminations against her for leaving me at a time like that. Ranting at *her* for—

Yes, with a girl as spirited as Geraldine, and who hated dishonesty as much as she hated it, I could see now why my answer to that letter had come from Reno.

There was a shred of doubt left. Only a shred; the story I was hearing made too horrible sense *not* to be true, otherwise. It fitted; Geraldine's being released by kidnapers and then walking out on me, knowing or being able to figure out why I'd perjured myself, *didn't* fit. But—

I asked, "Why did Dixie have that second note left? Once he'd been set free, they couldn't try him again. What did it matter to him whether Geraldine knew why I'd done—what I did do?"

The man across the table said, "I told you that at the start. Dixie hated your guts."

I stood up slowly and pushed my chair back. I said, "And now Dixie's got her again? No, I don't mean *again;* I mean he really kidnaped her. Why? In God's name, why?"

He said, "Sit down, Bonnert. No, Dixie hasn't got her. *I* have." And then he must have seen my eyes, for he talked fast: "If anything happens to me, she dies, Bonnert. And besides that, I've got a gun in my pocket, under the table. I can shoot before you could—"

I said, "Who the hell are you and what do you want? If you know all that about me, you know I'm broke and on the bum. You know no copper in town would take my word for—"

"I know all that," he said. "What I want, you can do. It ought to be a pleasure, Bonnert. *I want you to kill Dixie Wilman.* And my name, if you're interested, is Morelli."

II

I got it then. Of course I'd heard of Duke Morelli. Everybody in town had heard of Morelli, although he'd been there only a few months. He'd come in on the ground floor, somehow, as Dixie Wilman's right-hand man. How, nobody knew exactly. Maybe he'd bought his way in. Maybe Wilman had sent for him from somewhere or had known him before. Probably the department had the inside story on where Morelli had come from and why, but I wasn't in the department any more. All I knew was what I heard in casual conversation.

But Dixie Wilman had picked wrong; that was obvious. Morelli wanted Wilman killed so he could take over.

I stared at him. "But why *me?*" I asked him. "You've got torpedoes, or can get them. I'm no killer."

"I heard you were handy with a heater, Bonnert. That you got into several gun fights and came out standing up."

"That was different, Morelli. Those were guys I was trying to arrest, and they resisted and said it with lead. But—man, for five hundred bucks you could get a torpedo here from Chi that'd—"

"I don't want a torpedo from Chi," he said. "I want you. I want you so bad I took the risk of a kidnaping to get you. And there's five grand in it—if you come out alive."

I had to have time to think. There wasn't any way out of this without thinking. It wouldn't do me any good to take Morelli, even if I could. I called across to Joe to bring me another cup of coffee, and then I said to Morelli:

"Any objection to telling me why you'd rather pay me five thousand than somebody else five hundred?"

"None at all," he said. "Look, I could have Dixie rubbed out so the cops couldn't prove who did it. But the gang would know, and some of them wouldn't like it. Some of them like Dixie better than me, see? There'd be a split, maybe a fight. The racket wouldn't hold together, not without some other killings. Maybe enough to clamp down on pinball till none of us could operate."

I said, "But what's the difference whether it's me or some-body else, unless I do it openly. And if—"

Joe was walking over with the coffee, and I stopped. I gave Joe my last nickel.

When Joe was out of hearing, Morelli said, "You're getting the idea. I want you to kill Dixie openly. You got motive to do it, and if Dixie is bumped off by an outsider like you, I can take over quietly. No trouble. Nobody'll know I had anything to do with it."

"The two hoods in the car—didn't they know who Geraldine is?"

"They're on my side. They came here with me."

I took a drink of the coffee, hot, black and unsweetened. It burned like hell going down. But there were other things inside me that burned worse. Worst, maybe, was the knowledge that Geraldine *hadn't* left me flat just because I was in disgrace. She'd thought—well, I hated to think what she'd thought, reading those stories in the newspapers and not hearing from me except that one damn letter in which I was mostly mad at her for doing something she hadn't done, and which gave her the wrong idea entirely.

And I'd misjudged her and stayed away. If I'd gone where she was, a few minutes' talk would have—Wait, Larry, I told myself. No use thinking about that now. Geraldine's in a jam. Worry about the past later. Her only chance is if you at least pretend to play along with Morelli.

I put down the coffee mug and asked him, "What's the play? How am I supposed to kill him openly and get away with it? Or am I?"

He said, "You can get away with it. But you'll have to lam afterward. You'll have to live somewhere else, with a new name. But you'll have five grand when you get there. That isn't hay. And you'll have your wife—your ex-wife."

"Tell me the set-up," I told him. "When and where and how."

"*When* is tonight. Dixie's giving a party for the gang tonight at his place. A stag. All of us'll be there, and by midnight everybody'll be well oiled, see? That's when you walk in and burn down Dixie. If you haven't a heater, buy one out of that fifty bucks."

"Just shoot him," I said sarcastically, "and walk out again, with his gang there. Most of them heeled. Just shoot him down and say, 'Well, so long, boys; sorry I got to go'?"

Morelli grinned.

"Not *quite* that bad. Most of them won't be heeled. It's a party and nobody looking for trouble. And I'll be there, and a couple of *my* boys who'll be in on the play. You shoot and run, and we'll be the first to go after you, but we'll get in the way of any of the others that do. Leave the motor running on your car, and—"

"What car?"

"The town is full of cars," said Morelli. "Can't you pick a lock?"

"When and where do I get the money—and my wife?"

"After you shoot your way out of Dixie's, tonight, you lam to Cincinnati. You can make it in six hours' drive. Check in at the Haviland Hotel there; use the name Walter Burke. We'll bring you the girl and the money."

He was lying, but I nodded. There was one thing clear; I'd never get out of Dixie's tonight. Morelli and his men would wait until I'd shot Dixie and then—if someone else hadn't—they'd burn me down. The cops would thank them for it, under the circumstances, and the men in Dixie's gang who were loyal to Dixie would trust Morelli if he played it that way. And there wouldn't be anyone to implicate Morelli, either. There wouldn't be me. And there wouldn't be Geraldine, either.

I knew all that, but I had to play along until there was an out. I had to pretend to be a sucker.

I said, "You've got the cards, Morelli. And plugging Dixie Wilman will be a pleasure. But I'm making two conditions."

"You're not in a position to make any—"

"Nuts," I said. "I'm in a position to tell you to go to hell, unless you convince me I'm going to get Geraldine back. When I lam, I want to take her with me, and that means she's got to know what's going on. I want to see her now."

"She knows what's going on," he said, and something in his face made me think he was telling the truth. "You don't have to see her. Why should we risk—"

"The other one," I told him, "is in your favor, Morelli. Look, I may have to shoot my way out tonight. You admit it. I want to know which two boys at the party are on your side, so I don't burn them down by mistake. I don't want to give you excuse to renege. And you don't want them shot, do you?"

"You saw them, in the car with—"

"One I didn't see at all. He was behind my wife—my ex-wife. The other, the one who drove, I got a casual look at. I'm not sure I'd know him again. That car was in sight for only seconds, Morelli. They swung out from the curb the instant I turned."

He looked at me for a long time, and I could see he was thinking it over. I knew that second condition would make sense to him, and I was hoping it would carry the first.

I said, "I'd kill Dixie for free, after what you told me. But five grand isn't enough to make me kill him openly and be a fugitive the rest of my life. I got to be sure Geraldine will want to come back to me. Only for that—"

Finally he grunted and stood up. He said, "Wait here a few minutes after I've gone. Then go to the corner of Spring and Grand, and wait there. Alone. We'll pick you up around six."

I nodded, and I went back to eating while he walked out. There were four rolls in front of me now; the two that had come with Morelli's coffee and the two that had come with mine. They tasted like sawdust, but I ate all of them.

Joe strolled over. He said, "Everything O.K., Larry?"

"Everything's swell, Joe," I told him. "Tonight is the end of something. I don't know what. I'm—"

I started to say I was glad, but I didn't. For myself I would have been glad, whatever happened. But they had Geraldine.

I said, "I want to buy a gun, Joe."

"I got a .38 in the drawer under the cash register. Revolver. It's an old one, but—"

"It's what the doctor ordered, Joe," I told him. "How much?"

"You don't need to buy it. I'll lend it to—"

"Nothing doing. Twenty-five bucks O.K.?"

"Hell, yes, but—"

I took the fifty out of my pocket and gave it to him. I said, "Make out a bill of sale, to protect yourself, Joe. Just in case."

He shrugged and went back of the counter, and from there into the back room. He came back in a few minutes and passed me the gun under the table and then counted out twenty-five dollars in fives and ones on top of the table.

He said, "Don't worry about the bill of sale. I bought that in a Brooklyn hock shop eight years ago. It couldn't be traced to me."

"Swell," I said. "It's loaded?"

Joe nodded. I stood up, and for some fool reason I shook hands with him.

He said, "Larry, is there anything I can do?"

"Nothing," I told him. There wasn't a thing I could tell him that it wouldn't get him in trouble to know. Maybe with the police, maybe with the other side. I didn't know yet how I was going to play this, except that if there wasn't any out before midnight, I was going to use my second shot on Morelli. The hoods under him might have less reason to kill Geraldine if Morelli wasn't around.

It was a quarter of six, and it would take me ten or fifteen minutes to get to Spring and Grand. I went there and waited.

At a few minutes after six, a big sedan swung in to the curb and stopped. It was the same car that had stopped in front of the restaurant. The same man was driving, and Morelli and the man who'd sat next to Geraldine were in the back seat.

I opened the door and got in, between them.

I said, "I bought the gun. It's in my right coat pocket. You'd better—"

"We'll take good care of it, pal," said Morelli. And to the man behind the wheel: "O.K., Pete. Some quiet spot." The car started. Morelli said to me, "These boys will be on your side. They'll get in the way of anybody who starts after you, accidental-like. Don't shoot at them. Don't shoot anybody you don't have to, except Dixie; I want somebody left to work with."

I said, "O.K., I know them now. And now I want to see—"

"We're taking you there."

III

The car headed north out of town, and swung off the road into the driveway of what was obviously a deserted farmhouse. A gun appeared in Morelli's hand the moment we were off the main road, and he jammed it into my ribs.

He said, "This isn't it. This is just a stop-over."

The car turned behind the empty house, where it was out of sight of the road. The man on my right took the gun out of my pocket, and then tied a thick blindfold around my eyes.

Morelli said, "Down on the floor. We'll put the blanket over you. From here on you don't see where you're going."

I didn't argue; I got down on the floor of the car. I didn't mess with the blindfold, even though my hands were free and

the blanket was over me. I knew they'd check it when we stopped again, before they let me put my head up where I could
see anything.

I kept track of directions as we backed into the driveway,
went out to the road again, and turned south, back toward
town.

But pretty soon we turned again, and again, and I lost track.
My ears stayed on the job, though, and I knew we didn't go
through any heavy traffic. Most of the time, too, we were on roads
rather than streets. Then there was a long stretch of winding road that went mostly uphill, and we stopped. It had been,
as near as I could guess, half an hour from the time we'd stopped at the empty farmhouse.

I knew that where we were now was in the general direction
of north of the city; there wouldn't have been time for them to
cut through to the other side. And I knew we weren't back at
the farmhouse again because of the winding road and the
uphill stretch. It was a little knowledge, but not much.

Morelli—or the other guy—pulled the blanket off me and
examined the blindfold. Then, with a gun in my back they took
me along an unpaved path and through a door. I heard Morelli's voice say, "Be sure all the shades are down, here—and in
there." And a minute later he said, "Pete, you go outside and
watch the window in the other room. We'll give the guy a break.
We'll give him a few minutes alone with her."

The door opened and closed, and then Morelli took off my
blindfold. We were in a big room that looked like a hunting
lodge, with trophies on the wall. There were several windows,
but the shades were pulled down tightly.

Morelli stepped back with the blindfold in one hand and a
gun, aimed at me, in the other. The other man who'd been in
the back seat of the car had a gun in his hand, too, and stood
six feet off in another direction. There wasn't a chance in a
billion for a break.

Morelli jerked his head to a door on one side of the room. He said, "She's in there, Bonnert, and you can have a few minutes with her. She isn't hurt. She's tied up and you leave her that way, because otherwise we'll have to do it over again before we go. But you can take the tape off her lips so you can talk with her. We gave her some dope, just a little, when we took her to the outside of the restaurant, but she ought to be out of that by now. All right, what you waiting for?"

I didn't know what I was waiting for. The thought of *her* behind that door—

I'd hated her for a year. I'd thought I'd hated her. And she had hated me. Or thought she'd hated me.

I got my legs moving and I went into the room and closed the door behind me. She was lying on the bed, her wrists and ankles tied, and the rope that tied her wrists tied to the bed itself. And adhesive tape over her lips. I saw all that as I flicked the light switch on the wall just inside the door.

She was conscious, and her eyes blinked in the sudden light in a room that had been dim with twilight, and then they met my eyes, and in them I read all I wanted to know. Even before I took the adhesive tape—as gently as I could—off her lips, I knew that she loved me still, or again, and that she knew now the truth of what had happened a year ago.

I kissed her and said—Well, never mind everything I said to her or everything she said to me in those few minutes we had together.

Then I went to the window and looked out through the narrow slit between the edge of the shade and the window frame. It didn't mean anything. Just trees, gray in the dusk. The window itself was locked.

I could have unlocked it, of course, or jumped through the

glass, but Pete was waiting outside there, with a gun trained on the window. Morelli thought of everything.

I was back talking to Geraldine when Morelli opened the door.

He said, "O.K., come on."

Pete came back in while I was in the outer room, and he and the other hood kept me covered while Morelli went in and put adhesive over her lips again and checked that I hadn't tampered with the ropes.

Then the blindfold went back over my eyes and they drove me back—by what seemed to be approximately the same route—to the empty farmhouse again. And from there, openly, back to the same corner where they'd picked me up.

Morelli said, "I'm giving you your gun back now. But don't get any bright ideas. She dies just the same if—by any miracle —you got all three of us before we could get you. I've arranged for that."

He grinned, "Besides, we'll hand you the gun after you're outside, and this car is bulletproof."

I got out of the car, and the guy who'd taken the gun from my pocket closed the door, then lowered the glass an inch from the top and handed the gun through the slit. I put it in my pocket. Even if Morelli was lying when he said he'd made arrangements for Geraldine to die, I couldn't have got all three of them.

Morelli said, "See you at midnight."

The car drove off and left me standing there.

It was around eight o'clock. I had four hours to kill—if I was following orders—except that I had to steal, rent, or borrow a car.

At midnight I could go to Dixie's. I could shoot down Dixie and try to make a getaway, hoping that Morelli was playing straight with me. There was a chance in a hundred that he was.

Or I could *try* to burn down Dixie, Morelli, and the two men of Morelli's who probably had orders to shoot me as soon as I'd taken care of Dixie. And then to get away from the others—there'd be at least a dozen of them there—and to find my wife before anything happened to her.

There was a chance I could do that. But my mathematics weren't adequate to figure the chances against it. I don't know, offhand, what comes next after quadrillions and quintillions.

I went back to Joe's. I said, "Joe, I'm going to steal your car, O.K.?"

"The gas tank's full," said Joe. "But don't trust the brakes too far. Here's the key."

"No," I told him. "I can start it without the key. You protect yourself and report it stolen. Just one thing I want you to do; don't miss it or call the police till after midnight."

"I wouldn't anyway. I'll be here till around one o'clock. Sure you want me to report it then?"

"Positive," I told him. "This. . .this mess will be over one way or the other at midnight. If I'm alive I'll bring your car back; if I'm not the police will find it on the street somewhere."

"Luck," said Joe. "But you sure you can handle this yourself? Hadn't you ought to go to the cops?"

"I would, if I knew—"

Joe said, "I saw that car stop out front before. With the two men and the girl in it. Was the girl—wait, that's none of my business. But I've seen the two mugs before. One's named Pete Carey, and the other they call Chuck; I don't know the rest of his name."

"Thanks, Joe," I said. "That might help. Thanks for everything."

I went out the front way and walked around the block to the parking lot in back and got his car started.

Yes, knowing the names of the two mugs who were on Morelli's side just might help. If I could parlay that information.

And Joe was right that I should go to the cops. But I pictured myself walking into the station—me, with the reputation I had down there now as a crooked copper and a drunken bum. With the yarn I'd have to hand them they'd keep me there questioning me, or maybe they'd kick me out before I got through talking.

Then I thought of Cap Flinders. He'd give me a hearing if anybody would, and he knew more about the Wilman-Morelli mob than anyone else on the force. And he'd be off duty now; if I could catch him alone at his place—

I drove there, and I didn't spare the horses under the hood of Joe's car. I knocked on the door and Flinders opened it.

I said, "Cap, I've got to talk to you. It's important."

"Police business?" he asked coldly.

"Yes."

"Go down to the station, then, and talk to somebody on duty. Whatever it is, Bonnert, I wouldn't believe a damn word—" he was starting to close the door.

I put my weight against the door and slammed it back open, which threw him off balance. I went on in and pulled the gun out of my pocket and leveled it at him so he wouldn't get any ideas. For the moment his low opinion of me would help; he'd think I really meant my threat with the gun.

I kicked the door shut behind me, and said, "I said this was important. Morelli's kidnaped Geraldine. My price for getting her out of it is to burn down Dixie Wilman so Morelli can take over."

He leaned against the wall and looked at me sourly. "That sounds likely. Your ex-wife isn't even in town. I heard she hasn't seen you since—"

"I don't care what you think," I told him. "I came here to get some information, if you got it. You'll tell me or I'll knock it out of you. Does Morelli own a hunting lodge, or any place like a hunting lodge within an hour's drive of the middle of town?"

He stared at me a moment, puzzled at the question. Then he said, "Can't see any reason why I shouldn't answer that, or I wouldn't. As far as I know, Morelli doesn't own or rent any real estate except his suite at the—"

"Pete Carey?"

"Um·m·m·no. But that other rat Morelli brought here with him, Chuck Evans. He's got a place. I don't think he knows we know about it. He rented it for the season under the name of James Wheeler."

I found I was hardly breathing. It couldn't be this easy. I started to ask the next question and my voice cracked, and I had to take a breath and start over.

I said, "Is it north of town?"

"Northwest."

"You go up a hill just before you get there? Winding road, gravel path from where you'd park a car? One big room with rough·cut oak flooring and a stone fireplace, and two small bedrooms opening off it, and a deer head with the glass eyes set in a little crooked over the mantel?"

He said, "I didn't notice the deer's eyes. The rest fits."

"That's where they're holding Geraldine," I said. "You've got to take me there!"

He said, "You're probably lying, but I don't see why you would be. And you were a good guy once. All right, come on. And put that gun back in your pocket. You won't need it, for me."

I waited until he took off his coat and put on a shoulder holster, and then we got in Joe's car. I let Cap Flinders drive it. He said, "I'll work—for now—on the assumption you're telling the truth. It's almost too screwy not to be true. So there might be a mob of them there; hadn't we better get some of the boys on our way through town?"

I shook my head. "There's a big party at Dixie's tonight. Most, if not all, of them will be there. That partie's where I got a date at midnight. But it'll be a different kind of date if—"

It was nine o'clock when we got out of town. Flinders put on the brakes for the first crossroad, and went right through it. He said, "You better get this can fixed, Bonnert."

"It isn't mine," I said. "I stole it, for tonight."

He took his eyes off the road long enough to look at me. He said, "Damn if I don't think you're leveling."

"Get some more speed out of this thing," I told him. "How much longer?"

"Fifteen minutes."

I said, "That's enough time. Listen, Cap, I'm going to tell you what this is all about—tonight, and a year ago. You can take it or leave it." And I told him.

IV

We started up a winding hill, and then turned off the road into a long uphill driveway. In the moonlight, I could see the outline of a one-story building that looked like it could be the one. It had to be the one. There weren't any lights on.

I opened the glove compartment of the car to see if there was a flashlight, and there was. With it in one hand and the revolver in the other, I started running up the gravel path before Flinders could get out of the car. There wasn't any use being quiet; if anyone was there, they'd have heard the car coming up the drive.

The door was locked. I kicked my way in through a window, and it was the right place. There was no one there in the main room. I didn't wait to turn on the lights or open the door for Flinders; I just ran like hell for the little room on the left.

A moment later, I was untying her.

Flinders must have followed me through the window; he was standing in the doorway now. He said, "Is. . . is she all right, Larry?" It was the first time in a year that any member of the police force had called me by my first name.

Geraldine herself answered him.

I almost carried her out to the car because her legs were partly numb from having been tied so long. We didn't talk much on the way back to town, but we said enough to fix things up between us. And I knew that this time they'd stay fixed.

Over her objections we left her at the Samaritan Hospital. There was nothing wrong, the doctor said, that a good night's sleep and a day's rest thereafter wouldn't fix.

I didn't tell her about my midnight date; I got away on the plea that I had to go to headquarters with Flinders to make a deposition about the kidnaping.

Back in the car, Flinders said, "Now we'll get the boys and pick up Morelli's trio. With your wife's testimony, we got him."

"How about Dixie?"

He slowed down a little. "What do you mean, how about Dixie?"

"We haven't anything on him. Sure, now I can reverse my testimony on that charge of a year ago, but he's been tried and freed on that charge. We can't bring it again—and he wasn't in on this."

"But we can get him on. . .on conspiracy. Those times your mail box was frisked, the note that was written—"

"I haven't got the note any more. We haven't any proof but Morelli's word, and Morelli wasn't even in town then. We can't frame any charge against him that would stick."

Flinders shrugged. "So we can't hold him, then. But he'll slip sometime!"

"He'll slip tonight. Cap, I'm keeping that date."

"You're crazy. If you think we're going to let you go there to commit murder, you're crazy."

"I'm crazy," I said, "But I'm not going to commit murder. Listen." And I talked hard and fast for the ten minutes it took us to reach the station.

He said, "It's too risky. Larry, we'll try to get you reinstated, and we'll give you the assignment, again, of getting something on—"

"Nuts," I said. "It was my testimony that let Dixie out of a legitimate murder rap. I don't *want* reinstatement, while he's running loose. That's something I've got to take care of before I can look the boys in the face again. And my idea'll work, Cap."

I took out the .38 revolver I'd bought from Joe, and I swung out the cylinder and emptied the cartridges into my palm and handed them to Flinders.

"Here you are, Cap," I told him. "*Loaded,* this gun could take care of six mugs. But *empty—you* watch."

"I can't let you do it, Larry. It's too—"

"What time is it?"

He glanced at his wrist watch. "Almost eleven."

"Swell," I said. "Now shut up and don't argue. G'wan in and get the boys, and throw a cordon around Dixie's place like I told you. If I haven't come out by midnight, you can go in and take Morelli."

He growled, "And maybe pick up what's left of you. Larry, it's too damn risky. We don't want Dixie that bad."

"I do," I said. I'd slid behind the wheel when he stepped out of the car, and before he could argue any more I gunned it away from the curb and left him standing there.

I drove out Hayden Boulevard to Dixie's place. Not too slow, because I wanted to get there ahead of the cops. And not too fast, because I didn't want to get there too far ahead of them.

I knew Dixie's house well, inside and out, from the time I was working on him. It's a big twelve-room house set well back from the street and with plenty of yard on all sides of it. I parked in front, which was still a hundred yards from the house, and got out of the car and tiptoed across the grass instead of the path.

I figured it wasn't eleven thirty yet, and Morelli wouldn't be looking for me for a half-hour yet. And Dixie wouldn't be looking for me at all. But just the same, I walked as quietly as I could and took advantage of all the cover there was.

There were lights on in all the downstairs rooms. A radio was blaring in one room and a phonograph in another, and there was the click of poker chips and the faint rattle of dice and the clinking of ice in glasses.

There were at least a dozen men in there; Morelli's estimate of that had been conservative. And I didn't hear any women's voices; I was glad of that, although I'd have gone ahead just the same if they'd brought their women.

I went around to the back, made sure that the windows above the back porch were dark, and that nobody was looking out the window downstairs that commanded the porch. Then, as quickly as I could, I shinned up the post of the porch and made its roof. A minute later I was in the house, upstairs, and I'd made it without being seen.

The room I was in was a bedroom. I left the window wide open for a quick exit, and I put my empty revolver down on the porch roof just outside the window where it wouldn't be visible unless someone stuck his head out of the window and looked straight down.

Then I crossed the room to the door that led to the lighted upstairs hallway. I listened carefully at the door before I opened it a crack. Through that crack, I could see the head of the stairway, and the bathroom was just opposite the head of the stairs. With the boys drinking heavily, there'd be frequent trips up those stairs.

I waited maybe ten minutes and then the first one who came up was Pete Carey, Morelli's henchman. I didn't want him, so I kept back out of sight.

He went back down, and the next one to come up, a few minutes later, was Baldy Wacker. He'd do, for what I had in mind. He'd been with Dixie for years, and he'd definitely be on Dixie's side against Morelli. As soon as he reached the head of the stairs, I stepped out of the bedroom into the hall and said, "P·s·s·t. Baldy!"

He had a gun in his hand almost before he'd turned around to see who I was. I kept my own hands carefully out from my body so he'd be sure I wasn't going for a gun, and I said softly, "Yeah, it's me, Baldy. C'mere. It's important."

There was suspicion all over his rather dumb face, but he had a gun in his hand and I didn't, so he came over closer.

I said softly, "Listen, Baldy, I got some information that's important to Dixie. I got to get it to him without any of the rest of the gang hearing. He'll pay me big for it, but I had to come in this way, so the others wouldn't—"

"What information?"

I said, "Morelli's making plans to kill Dixie and take over. He's got some of the boys with him and I'm not sure which— but I know it wouldn't be you. I can prove it to Dixie. I got to see him without the others knowing."

He grunted. "Since when you a particular friend of Dixie's?"

"The hell with that. I want money; he'll pay for what I know."

Baldy was close enough now that the gun was in my ribs. He said, "H'ist 'em. I want to be sure you ain't heeled."

I put up my hands and let him frisk me. He did a good job of it. And it must have convinced him, because he put his own gun back in his pocket.

He said, "I'll go down again and bring Dixie up here."

"No," I told him. "It's too risky here; I'm not sure who's on his side, and I don't want to be caught in here. I'm going out the way I came. Tell Dixie to come out the front door."

"How'd we know it ain't a trap?"

"Nuts," I said. "If I was laying for Dixie, I wouldn't have showed myself to you, would I? I'd have waited till he came upstairs himself. And I'd have brought a gun."

I got a break then that saved me having to argue any more. There were footsteps at the bottom of the staircase, coming up, and the guy was singing off key, and it was Morelli's voice.

I quickly whispered to Baldy, "I'm scramming. Tell Dixie to come out the front door and walk toward the big oak tree on the left. He can come heeled if he don't trust me."

Then I stepped back into the bedroom and pushed the door shut silently. I heard Morelli tell Baldy he'd better get back to the crap game; the boys wanted revenge.

I didn't wait around any longer. I slid through the window, retrieved my empty gun, and went down the porch post and around to the front, behind the oak tree which was a good forty yards from the front of the house.

I waited there, and about five minutes later the front door opened and Dixie Wilman came out. I hadn't seen him for a year, but he hadn't changed any; he was as squat and ugly and gnomelike as he was a year ago, and he didn't look any older. He strolled down the path toward the tree where I waited, his hands in his pockets.

When he was a couple of yards away I stepped out where he could see me, and said, "Hello, Dixie."

My hands were at my sides, empty, but I'd shoved the revolver butt-first up my left sleeve and held it there with a slight
pressure of my wrist against my thigh. When I relaxed that
pressure the gun would drop into my hand. The empty gun.

He said, "What's this about Morelli?"

"Morelli tried to hire me to kill you. He wants to take over.
He wanted me for a fall guy because if he or one of his men did
it, it'd split the mob."

"Can you prove that?"

"Sure," I said. "This is plenty proof, right here." With my
right hand, moving slowly so he'd be sure I wasn't reaching for
a gun, I took a folded paper from my breast pocket and held
it out toward him.

He reached for it, and for that moment his hand was off his
gun. I let the empty revolver slide down into my left hand and
stepped in, jamming it into his ribs. The paper—a dun from
one of my creditors—fell to the ground between us.

Dixie's face turned pasty as his hands went up in reply to
the gun muzzle in his ribs. That had been the bad moment; if
he'd gone for his gun again, I'd have had to slug him, and my
plan would have foozled then and there.

I took his gun out of his pocket with my free hand and I
threw it so it landed on the grass half-way to the house. Then
I stepped back and shifted the revolver to my right hand.

I said, "You want proof, Dixie? I'll give it to you two ways.
First, Morelli told me how you framed me a year ago on that
kidnap stunt. He wanted me to have more reason than money
to kill you."

Dixie wet his lips with the end of his tongue. He asked,
"How much did Morelli offer? I'll give you—"

"The other proof," I said, "is that I took his offer. *I'm going
to kill you,* right now."

And I pulled the trigger. The gun clicked empty. I jerked the trigger again, trying to look frantic and horrified about it.

Dixie's face changed; he wheeled and ran for the gun I'd taken from his pocket and thrown away. I cursed and dropped mine, and ran for the car. I was in it, pulling out from the curb, when he recovered his automatic. I saw him look my way, and decide it was too far for a good shot. And he could take care of me later, he'd figure.

As I drove hastily away he turned and walked toward the house.

I left the car a few doors down and ran back to where I'd spotted Flinders and a couple of the boys behind a hedge. I said, "It worked, Cap. He's going in there for a showdown with Morelli. I convinced him all right."

Flinders said, "We got thirty men, all around the place. Do you think—"

"Dixie won't waste any time," I said. "He'll—"

From the house came the sound of a pistol shot, and then an irregular fusillade of shots. Flinders started to put his whistle to his lips, but I caught his hand.

"Let 'em shoot it out, Cap," I said. "The more of each other they kill, the less electricity we'll have to use on the ones that are left."

Flinders chuckled. He said, "It's a darb of a set-up. They're *all* going to be accessories, at least."

There was a lull in the shooting, one last shot, and then silence. That meant that Morelli and his men, who were outnumbered, wouldn't bother us any more. And it meant that those who were still alive of Dixie's wouldn't bother us much longer either. We'd have them cold.

Cap Flinders blew the whistle and the cordon closed in.

Geraldine had read the morning papers and they were scattered over her bed. Even in a hospital nightgown she looked beautiful. But she glared at me reproachfully.

"You . . .you utter fool," she said. "Taking a chance like that! It was—"

I kissed her, and then grinned.

"It was cowardly of me, honey," I said. "Now that I have to be a cop again. I didn't want to take any chances. While Dixie's mob ran things, it used to be *dangerous* to be on the force. But from now on—"

And then I quit trying to be funny and sat down on the edge of the bed and put my arms around her. I said, "Honey, I went around to find out, and we can get the same apartment back that we had before. Thank God it doesn't take as long to get remarried as it does to get divorced, and everything will be the—"

The same? No, I knew it wouldn't, and from her eyes I could see that she felt that way about it, too. Not the same, but a thousand times better. You have to lose something first and then, miraculously and unexpectedly, get it back, before you can begin to understand how much better.

DEATH'S DARK angel

You'd have liked Walter Hanson. Not admired him, maybe, because his best friend wouldn't have called him a hero. He was a good five inches shorter than Clark Gable and his ears stuck out even farther. He wasn't suave like Bill Powell, nor tough like Humphrey Bogart.

In fact—well, take your conception of the opposite of Humphrey Bogart, and you've got a pretty good picture of Walter Hanson. He wouldn't hurt a fly, and he was afraid of anything bigger than that. He was afraid of women, and afraid of the dark. But he was a nice guy, for the psychic shape he was in.

Maybe it was just as well he didn't know what he was headed for, that evening.

He was scared enough, as it was. It was pretty dark on the corner, with the street light out. Darned dark, for seven-thirty in the evening.

And the man standing back there in the doorway, wearing a gray topcoat and a gray slouch hat pulled down over his eyes, *did* look like Humphrey Bogart. Not only that, but there wasn't anybody else in sight and the man had his right hand thrust deep into the pocket of the topcoat.

Hanson hurried past and turned in at the door of "Slim" Wendorf's cigar store.

Wendorf was alone in the store. A tall man with a nose so thin and sharp-edged that you scarcely saw the rest of his features. His deep-set eyes looked broodingly at Walter Hanson over the counter.

"Uh—" said Hanson, "I came to collect my bet."

Wendorf didn't move. He stared at Hanson as though he had never seen him before, although he had, on at least half a dozen occasions. But those times Hanson had been making bets on horses which lost. Maybe it was different, now that a horse had won.

There was a sudden panic in Hanson's mind. What if Wendorf said, "Yeah, what bet?" Not that the amount was big, but what would he say if Wendorf said—

"Yeah," Wendorf said. "Whatsa name?"

"Hanson. Walter Hanson. I had a dollar on—"

"Just a minute."

The tall man turned his back and opened a drawer. He took out a slip of paper and squinted down at it.

"Yeah," he said. "Dark Angel, nine to one. Ten bucks ya got coming."

He pushed a key on the cash register, took a limp bill from the drawer, and put it on the counter.

"Uh—thank you," said Hanson, picking up the bill nervously. He felt he ought to say or do something more. "I—I'd like some cigarettes, please. A carton of Vegals."

Wendorf bent over and peered through the glass of the counter. There were cigarettes inside, but except for a few leading brands, the boxes were dusty. The only carton of Vegals was open and there were only two packs left in it.

"Got some in back," Wendorf said. "Wait a minute."

He went through the door to the back room.

Walter looked at the bill in his hand, wondered whether to pay for the cigarettes out of it or use a couple of the singles in his wallet. Maybe he should keep the ten intact, for luck. It was the biggest bet he had ever won.

He took out his wallet and started to put the ten-dollar bill in it, then hesitated. There was "Humphrey Bogart" outside and two doors away, waiting. Maybe he was a holdup man, waiting for somebody to come in here and collect a bet, come out and be held up.

Well, maybe not, but this *was* a bad neighborhood. At night, anyway. Hanson laid his billfold on the counter and, with a surreptitious look around, took off his hat and slipped the ten-dollar bill under the band, inside.

Not that he expected to be held up, of course, but if he should be, there would be only the singles in his billfold to lose. He heard footsteps in the back room and thought he heard a low murmur of voices. Maybe Wendorf was coming back. Hanson hastily put his hat back on and pretended to be staring interestedly at a card of cheap pipes hanging on the wall high behind the counter.

But Wendorf did not come back.

There was a noise like a thud behind the partition. For an instant Walter Hanson thought that Wendorf had fallen. Then there were footsteps again, and he was reassured.

A sound he could not quite identify, and then silence.

Long silence. Still Wendorf did not come back. The minutes ticked away. Hanson wished he could leave. He didn't really need those cigarettes. He had half a carton in his room.

He cleard his throat, then again, more loudly. He said:

"Uh—if you can't find them, Mr. Wendorf, just let it go. I'll—uh—get them some other time."

No answer. *Had* Wendorf fallen, maybe, and hurt himself? The door was ajar slightly. Walter Hanson walked back to it.

"Mr. Wendorf, are you all right?" he said, and pushed it a little wider.

The knob of the front door, behind him, rattled, and a bell rang somewhere as the door was pushed open. Hanson turned his head.

It was the man who looked like Humphrey Bogart. And there was another man with him now. A big man with a stupid, vicious face and thick, malformed ears. He wore a shabby brown topcoat that was too small for him, and a greasy gray cap.

"Hey, you," Humphrey Bogart said. Not loudly, but in just the kind of voice Hanson had known he would have. And Bogart's hand, from the knob of the door, darted toward the side pocket of his gray topcoat.

Hanson acted without thinking. He was too scared to think. He dived through the door in the partition and slammed it behind him. His momentum carried him into the back room, and he almost fell over the body on the floor.

The body of Slim Wendorf, the bookie. It lay there grotesquely sprawled, red, and spattered with blood. The throat was cut, deeply. Not a neat job of throat-slitting at all. It looked more as though his murderer, standing before him, had dealt a cross-handed blow with a saber. Inches deep it had gone, and there was blood over everything. Everywhere except inside the thing that had been Wendorf. There couldn't be any to speak of left inside him.

Walter Hanson was standing in splattered blood, staring down with horror that had made him for an instant forget what he was running from, when the knob of the partition door rattled. Then Bogart's voice said:

"Bust it down, Ears."

And there was a lunge against the door. The spring-lock held, but the whole partition shook. Heavy footsteps retreated, as for a run that would knock down the whole partition if the door held.

Hanson didn't wait. There was a back door, and it was ajar. He was through it and into the darkness of the alley when the door crashed.

The sound put wings on his feet, even through the dangerous dark. Footing was difficult on the rough cobblestones, but nevertheless, he ran. Toward the dimly silhouetted mouth of the alley, half a block away.

It was the sight of that area of comparative brightness that made him realize, before he had taken a dozen steps, that he would be a perfect target, running toward it.

There was a low fence to his left. Hardly breaking stride, he put his hands on it and vaulted over. The landing jarred him, for the hard-packed earth beyond the fence hit his feet unexpectedly soon. The yard was a foot higher than the alley.

He fell, and then there were voices in the alley and he lay where he had fallen, flat against the dirt and trying not even to breathe, lest a sound give him away.

"Which way'd he go, Smoot?"

It was a high-pitched voice, almost like a woman's. Hanson wondered if it could have come from the ugly giant with the cauliflower ears.

"Shut up, ya fool!" the voice of Bogart, whose name must be Smoot, growled.

For seconds there was utter quiet, as though they were listening. Then Smoot swore again.

"Ears," he said, "you get the car and drive around the block and then around the neighborhood. He can't be far. I'm going back in—in there."

"Gosh, Boss, the cops might—"

"Get going," Smoot's voice growled. "Worry about what Kelsey's gonna say, not the cops. Us watching the joint and this mug goes in and croaks him. Ten Gee's the chief loses."

"But it ain't our fault, is it? We was to watch the joint so Slim didn't lam, not that nobody should come in and—"

"Shut up and get going."

A door slammed, and footsteps ran toward the other end of the alley. Heavy footsteps that would be those of "Ears." And a moment later there was the sound of a car starting up.

Walter Hanson waited another five minutes, or maybe ten, before he stood up. By now his eyes were used to the darkness and he could see the ash box next to him. He stared at it thoughtfully for a moment, then took off his cravenette and stuffed it into the ash box.

The man called Ears couldn't have had much of a look at him, and would be looking now for a man in a light coat. And his hat—it had been turned up at the brim. He turned it down all the way round, as Bogart-Smoot's had been. Not much of a disguise, but better than nothing.

Carefully, then, he made his way between the buildings to the street. He peered out of the areaway down the street and the headlights of a car were coming. He started to pull back, then noticed the little green light between and above them that indicated that the coming vehicle was a taxi.

He stepped out to the curb and waved. The cab was empty and it stopped. Hanson got in.

"Winters' Restaurant," he said. "It's on Oak Street, just this side of—"

"I know where it is."

The cabby threw the engine into gear and started. Hanson watched fearfully out the back window for signs of pursuit, but there were none. Ten blocks further on, he sighed and relaxed. He had made it. He would never go near that neighborhood again.

For a minute he wondered if he should phone the police and tell them there had been a murder. But they would find out anyway. And maybe they would think, as Bogart and the ex-pug had thought, that he had committed it. And anyway he would have to admit he had been collecting a bet, and that was illegal and maybe they would put him in jail.

Anyway, his name would get in the papers and Smoot and Ears would know who he was and where to find him. Hanson shivered a little at the thought of that.

Oh, he knew he should notify the police all right. But by the time they reached the restaurant, he had pretty well convinced himself that it would be better for everybody if he didn't. After all, he couldn't tell the police who was guilty, and his story might just confuse the issue.

Big Si Winters, behind the register on the cigar counter, grinned at him.

"Hi, Walter," he said. "Back already? You get hungry quick."

Hanson said, "Huh?" blankly, and then looked at the clock. It was only seven forty-five, and he had left here only an hour ago. It seemed hours ago.

"Just came in for pie and coffee," he said. "I—uh—didn't want desert before, but I was walking around and got hungry and—"

"Sure," said Si Winters. "I won't sell you two cups of coffee with a meal, so you walk around the block and come back for the second one. Sure. But it's all right if you're celebrating. How much did you put on that long-shot tip I gave you?"

"Uh—Dark Angel? Say, thanks. I bet a dollar. I—uh—"

Suddenly he remembered that it was Winters who had introduced him to Wendorf a few weeks ago, when the bookie had been eating here. And when the morning papers told that Wendorf had been killed about seven-thirty, fifteen minutes before he, Hanson, had, . . . And had Si Winters noticed him getting out of a taxi?

But the fat restaurant proprietor was chuckling.

"A dollar, Walter?" he said. "You'll never get rich that way. Me, I bet a sawbuck, and I don't work in a bank like you do." He shook his head in mock sorrow. "All that money lying around loose and you shoot the works and bet a buck."

"Any time I rob the bank," Hanson said, "I won't bet it on long shots. I—uh—got to remember to go around tomorrow and collect. What were the odds? Nine to one?"

"Nine to one," said Winters solemnly. "And that ain't hay. For ninety bucks profit, I get myself some more of these fancy rayon shirts. Can't tell it from silk, can you?"

Hanson eyed the splendor of the salmon-hued shirt, and smiled.

"Looks better'n silk," he said. "Bet your washline looks like a rainbow, Si. Say—how many times a day do you change 'em? You had on a bright green one when I left here an hour ago."

"You're color blind, Walter," Winters said. "Or having hallucinations. Which reminds me—how'd you come out on the draft board business? You were up for reclassification, weren't you?"

Hanson nodded. "But I haven't heard yet."

"Hope they let you in," Winters said, "so you can lick those Japs and get me real silk for my shirts again." He chuckled. "You're all the Army needs, Walter."

Something inside Walter Hanson winced, but he said: "You should talk. Some day they'll slice you in half and make two soldiers out of you."

"Or inflate me for a blimp. I beat you to that one. Now go on back and make goo-goo eyes at Marjorie while you eat your pie."

Hanson went on back to the counter and sat down. He wished he did have the nerve to—well, not to make goo-goo eyes at Marjorie, but to ask her for a date. Women always had scared him. Particularly beautiful ones.

And Marjorie Randall was beautiful, all right. Beautiful with a healthy out-of-door type of beauty that you don't often see in restaurants.

"Back already?" she said, and smiled.

And, as usual, Walter Hanson's face froze when he tried to smile back. But he managed to make his tone of voice light.

"Back already," he said. "For coffee, and what kind of pie do you have?"

"Apple or mince. The mince is better."

"The mince, then," said Hanson, wondering how he would manage to get it down, since he was full already. "And—uh—"

"Yes?"

"Uh—nothing," said Hanson. "Say, Si seems pretty cheerful tonight."

"He ought to be. Been grouchy as a bear all afternoon, and this is reaction."

She brought his order, punched a ticket for it, and seemed to wait for him to say something further. But he didn't, and Marjorie went to clear away the dishes left by another customer.

Hanson ate the pie slowly and was sorry he had ordered it. But the coffee put a warm spot in him and made him feel better.

Si Winters was busy on the phone when Hanson left, but Hanson had even change so that didn't matter. He put the ticket and fifteen cents on the rubber pad by the register and went on out.

A squad car was pulling into the curb.

"Oh, Lord!" Walter Hanson thought. "They've found out I—"

But he didn't run this time. He stood waiting for them to take him.

But the first man out of the squad car was Burke, and he merely waved at Hanson.

"Hi, Hanson," he said. "We're putting on the feed bag. Have something with us?"

"J-just did," Hanson told him. "Uh—anything happening tonight?"

"Not much." Walter Hanson thought Burke looked at him a bit strangely, but that was probably imagination. "Filling station got held up, and a bookie got his throat cut. Both outa our district. Sure you don't want to have something with us? Pie and coffee, maybe?"

"No, thanks," Hanson told him. "I got to get home because—well, I got to get home."

And he started there, realizing that there was not a reason on earth why he had to except that there wasn't any place else he could think of to head for. But he had gone only a step when he remembered something he wanted to ask.

"Uh—Lieutenant. Did you ever hear of anybody named Kelsey?"

"Kelsey Deane?"

"I guess so," Walter said. "I just heard his first name."

"Short, stocky guy with a wart on his nose? Dresses like a Christmas tree?"

"I didn't see him. Just heard of him. Who is he?"

"One of the town's two-bit gangsters. Nobody important—but we'd like him out of the way if we could get something on him. Why?"

"I—I just heard somebody talking about him, and wondered," said Hanson. "That's all."

As he walked home, he tried to remember just what Smoot *had* said. Something like, "Worry about what Kelsey's going to say, not the cops. Us watching the joint and somebody goes in and croaks him." And then something about the boss—which was probably Kelsey, too—losing ten G's.

It didn't make much sense, but what sense it did make wouldn't indicate that Kelsey had killed Slim Wendorf. Not if he'd had his two henchmen, Smoot and Ears, watching Wendorf's place. So there wasn't any point, much, in telling the police what he had heard. If it had indicated who might actually have killed the bookie, that would be different.

There was a car parked across the street from the rooming house where Hanson lived. For a moment, he thought it was Si Winters' car—it was a big, expensive one of the same model— but then he saw it was not. And it was empty.

He went into the dimly lighted hallway and closed the door behind him. Home safely now, and he found he was trembling just a little, from delayed reaction, possibly. He stood still a moment until the trembling passed.

Then he picked up the half dozen letters still lying on the hall table and shuffled through them. Two of them were for him. One would be the receipt for his insurance premium.

The other was—*it*.

He opened it and read it through, reading the words as though seaching for a hidden meaning among them. As though they ought to tell him, somewhere, just where he would be sent, to fight whom, and how, and whether or not he was coming back afterward.

But the letter didn't tell him any of those things, and after he had put it back into the envelope and into his pocket, all of it he could really remember was the induction date, a week ahead.

He took a deep breath and walked up the stairs. He opened the door of his room, walked in and flicked on the light.

They were sitting there. Three of them.

"Don't make a noise, pal," Smoot said.

There was a gun in his hand. The big one with the cauliflower ears started to say something, but Smoot turned to glare at him and he subsided.

The third man was stocky and had a wart on his nose. He wore a suit that looked expensive, but too loud.

"Frisk the guy," he said. "If he's got it on him, we won't have to—"

Almost before he had finished speaking, Smoot was on one side of Walter Hanson and Ears was on the other. Ears ran a hand over him first.

"He ain't heeled," he said in a surprised way. "And he ain't got the shiv on him, either. If it was a shiv he used. Looked more like a—"

"Shut up, Ears," said the stocky man in the loud suit.

Smoot was searching thoroughly. He emptied Hanson's pockets, tossing their contents onto the bed. He felt linings. He found the ten-dollar bill under the hatband, looked at it disgustedly and tossed hat and bill together on the bed.

"Not on him, Chief," he said at last. "He stashed it. He had on a coat, too, when we saw him, and left that somewhere. Shall we work on him?"

"No," said Kelsey. "I think we can do this peaceable. Sit down, Hanson."

Walter Hanson sat down, gingerly, on the edge of the bed.

"Y-you seem to think I killed Wendorf," he said. "I didn't. I was just there collecting a—"

"Let me do the talking, Hanson."

Kelsey's voice was suave, but there was menace in it. He looked, Walter Hanson thought, like a smug, overdressed toad.

"You don't see why you should turn over that dough to us," he said, "and I don't blame you. I wouldn't want to, either. But I've got a right to ten grand of it, and I mean to have it. If you're reasonable, whatever's over that is yours. Ever hear of a horse called Dark Angel?"

"Sure. I bet on him, but—"

"I bet on him, too. A thousand on the nose. So I got nine grand coming from Wendorf, with my thousand back. See? I saw Slim right after the race, and he said he'd have the dough ready for me any time after seven-thirty tonight. But so Slim wouldn't get any ideas about welshing, and maybe take a powder instead of paying off, I had Sm—these two pals of mine watch the joint. And when you went in there and didn't come out, they went in and caught you red-handed. I don't know where you got the tip-off that Slim Wendorf was going to be heavy with dough this evening, and I don't care. See?"

"But I didn't—" Hanson began.

"Now, now, don't worry about that." Kelsey waved a pudgy hand. "You're among friends, as far as that little job goes. Slim's no loss, and we won't call copper on you. In fact, you ought to cut in on the job for saving your hide. You pulled a boneheaded trick."

"Yeah," said Smoot. "Amacher, if ya ask me. Look it." Grinning, he took a billfold from his pocket—Hanson's billfold—and tossed it on the bed. "Left your name and address lying on the counter! If I hadn't gone back in there to make sure the dough wasn't still there, you'd be entertainin' coppers right now, instead of us."

"And in this state," Ears said, "they fry ya till—"

"Shut up, Ears," said Kelsey. "Now listen, Hanson. I don't know how much you got off Wendorf and I don't care. But I want ten grand of it. Ain't that fair? Like he says, the coppers'd have you right now if it wasn't for us, and what good would the dough do you then?"

"Yes, but I haven't *got* it!" Hanson said. "I went there to collect a bet, a small bet, and I didn't—"

"Lemme work on him a while, Chief," Smoot said.

Kelsey puffed his thick lips out and drew them in again.

"Think it over, Hanson," he said. "We won't rush you. Give us ten grand, peaceable, and keep the rest. Or you'll end up without any of it."

"And six feet underground," said Smoot.

"But we work on you first," Ears said. "By the time you're dead, you'll be glad ya are."

Hanson looked wildly from one to the other of them.

"But I didn't kill Wendorf, I tell you!" he said. "Or rob him, either. So how can I—"

Kelsey sighed. "Smoot," he said, "is there any chance this guy's leveling?" His voice was bored and resigned.

"Slim was alive when this guy went in," Smoot said heavily. "Ten minutes later, I get wondering what he's doing so long, so I signal Ears and we go in. He's just coming outa the back room, Slim's laid out, and this guy lams the minute he sees us. Sure, he done it."

"Nobody else went in, meantime?"

"Nobody. Front or back. Ears was down by the end of the alley where he could see the back door. When I whistled, he came running around front."

"Somebody *did* come in the back way," Hanson said. "They must've. They could have got out while Ears was running around to the front, but—blast it, he must have been asleep or not watching when they went in."

Ears took a menacing step toward Hanson and raised a fist that looked as big as a ham.

"You're a liar!" he said. "I'll—"

"Sit down, Ears," said Kelsey.

"Don't call us liars, Hanson," Smoot said. "It's hard on the teeth. And get it over with. Do you kick in, or do we kill you?"

Kelsey leaned forward. "We give you ten minutes, Hanson. And that's all. Don't talk—unless you're going to tell us. Ears, stand there by him and slap his ears down if he pulls that "but I didn't—" line again."

"And if you take the full ten minutes," Smoot said, "we take the works or nothing. You don't get by with handing over ten grand."

Walter Hanson opened his mouth to speak, but couldn't think of anything that did not begin with "But I didn't—" so he closed his mouth again. At any rate, this was giving him time to think, if thinking could do him any good.

Tick of the clock on the bureau.

"Can I—now?" Ears said.

"Wait," Kelsey told him. Kelsey turned to Smoot. "You say he was wearing a coat? I'll bet he checked it somewhere, with the dough in it. Maybe we can work on that angle, if—" His tone of voice added, "If we have to kill him."

"Maybe," Smoot said. "But more likely he ditched it because he got blood on it. The way Slim's throat was slashed—"

Hanson's mouth popped open again. It was a wild idea, but it *could* be. Si Winters knew Wendorf. And Winters *had* been wearing a green shirt an hour before the murder. And he had denied changing it.

But Si Winters had money. He had a good restaurant, that made a good profit, and he had money in the bank. He himself handled Winters' account, and there was plenty in it. Nine or ten thousand in an account that jumped around a lot, up and down, but mostly up. Winters was not rich, but he was not broke by any means. Why would he want to kill a man for, . . . No, Si Winters as a robber didn't fit the picture.

But Winters' shirt had changed color from green to salmon. And maybe he would kill to keep from losing all he had. Suppose he was—

"Listen," Hanson said. "I got an—"

Ears' monstrous fist cocked back threateningly.

"Gonna tell us where you put the dough?"

"No, but I—"

"Shut up, then. You'll tell us that, or keep your trap shut till we shut it for you for good."

Kelsey glanced over his shoulder at the clock.

"And you better make up your mind pretty quick," he said.

Smoot reached down idly over the end of the bed and pawed through the things he had taken from Hanson's pocket.

"Might be a check-room stub or something," he said.

"You got two minutes," Kelsey said.

Hanson's eyes went to the clock. Behind him, he heard Smoot start to chuckle.

"I didn't read this before, Chief," Smoot said. "But look what's going in the Army next week. Or would be going in if he's still around to do it."

"This is your last chance, Hanson," Kelsey said. "And I'll throw in something. None of my boys get hooked, and I can fix it for you the same way. I know a— Well, never mind how, but I can fix that draft business for you. Is it a deal?"

Smoot chuckled. "Scared stiff. Boy, what a soldier our pal here would make!"

"Shut up, Smoot," Kelsey said. "All right, Hanson, you got a minute. But not a yip outa you unless it's a yes."

Tick of the clock on the bureau.

And Burke had said Kelsey was a two-bit gangster! A lot of things like that were going through Walter Hanson's head. Si Winters saying sarcastically, "You're all the Army needs." Kelsey, "None of my boys get hooked." Smoot's contemptuous "Scared stiff."

And what kind of a fighter *would* he make, against real opposition, if he couldn't figure an out against three two-bit gangsters like these?

But not here and now. With Ears' huge fist cocked back like

that, and with a gun in Smoot's hand, the odds were too heavy. He would have to stall. Maybe the squad car boys would still be inside the restaurant. Maybe even if they weren't—

"Okay," he said. "I'll take you where I hid the dough."

"Now you're being smart," Kelsey said. He stood up. "But don't let him pull anything on you, boys. One of you stay on each side of him. And if this is a gag—"

His eyes narrowed at Hanson. Then he went to the door, opened it.

"Come on," he said.

In the car, Kelsey drove, and Ears and Smoot sat one on each side of Walter Hanson in the back seat. Kelsey parked half a block away from the restaurant.

"Case the joint," he told Smoot. "And leave the rod with me. Even with Ears here, I'm not taking any chances on sonny boy."

Smoot went away, came back and nodded. "Not a customer in the place."

"No funny stuff now," Kelsey said.

"He won't pull anything," Smoot said. "We can handle him."

As Kelsey got out of the car, Smoot took the gun from him. He put it into his pocket, but kept his hand there.

The four of them went into the restaurant. Si Winters, behind the cigar counter, looked up at Walter.

"Back *again*?" he said, but his eyes were wary.

Marjorie was still on duty, Hanson saw. He had hoped she would be through her shift by now. But she was working at the coffee urn, way at the back.

Hanson stepped up to the cigar counter and the others pressed close behind him.

"Well?" Kelsey said.

Hanson jerked a thumb at Winters. "He's got it."

"Got what?" Winters demanded.

"The ten grand Wendorf owes Kelsey on the bet," Hanson

said. "Si, you were *backing* Wendorf. You and he thought Dark Angel was too long a shot to come home, and you let him take heavy money. But when the horse won, it would have broke you to pay off. And only Wendorf knew you were behind him. With him dead, you thought Kelsey here could whistle for his money and you'd be in the clear.

"With Wendorf alive, you couldn't welsh. He'd have given you away—or done you in, himself. You told him you'd call at seven·thirty with the money. You had the back door key to his place. And you took a butcher knife from the kitchen here and—"

The high·pitched voice of the big man with the califlower ears cut in.

"Him?" Ears said. "I saw him go back in the alley, but I'd seen him around there often and thought he lived around there. So I didn't think anything of it, Boss, or notice where he turned in. Good gee, was I a—"

"Shut up, Ears," said Kelsey. And whether or not the accusa·tion Walter Hanson had just made meant anything to the gangster or not, Ears' impromptu comment had registered. He stared at Si Winters over Hanson's shoulder.

"Well, Fatty?" he said.

Smoot's hand came out of his pocket with the gun in it, and rested on the glass of the counter, aiming at Winters.

It was Winters' move, then, but Walter Hanson didn't wait for it. His hands were resting on the edge of the counter, be·hind the gun. He raised them suddenly and smashed down·ward on top of the automatic.

The showcase glass crashed as the gun was driven through it.

The gun roared, coincidentally with Smoot's startled yell as glass cut deeply into his hand and wrist, but the bullet went downward into the cigar boxes below.

Hanson pushed himself away from the counter, throwing Kelsey and Ears, who had been close behind him, staggering back away from him. He whirled around. Ears was starting for him, his stupid face murderous, but Kelsey was in Ears' way, and Hanson swung for Kelsey, clipping him back of the ear with a rabbit punch, as his other hand went to his pocket for his cigarette case, to grasp in his other fist for purchase.

Behind him, a gun roared. Then another, or the same one again, and there was an appalling crash of glass and the floor shook.

Hanson hit Kelsey again, with the heavy cigarette case wrapped in his fist, and stepped in behind the blow to keep Kelsey between himself and Ears. Over his shoulder he got a glimpse of Si Winters, a revolver by his outstretched hand, fallen through the glass counter. And Smoot holding the automatic ready for another shot at Winters, in a hand that was red and dripping with blood.

Pain and rage contorted Smoot's face, and his left hand was pressed against his forward-bent body just over the diaphragm. And there was blood on that hand, too, running between the spread fingers. He could easily have shot Hanson, and the space was clear between them, but instead he stood there pumping shot after shot from the bloody gun into Si Winters' body. The last shot in the gun went wild as Smoot's legs crumpled under him.

But Walter Hanson couldn't watch that. He kept driving forward into Kelsey. Kelsey staggered back, and another push sent him into Ears.

Hanson bent down for the revolver Winters had dropped, and his fingers closed around it just as Ears, with a roar, got free of Kelsey and charged. He managed to trigger the gun once before Ears' fist him. It was a glancing blow, but it sent him sprawling backward across the floor.

Ears came on, grabbing a chair from one of the side tables. Hanson pulled the trigger again just as the chair reached the top of its swing. And the rage died out of the thug's face and it became even blanker and more stupid, as he stood there immobile a moment. Then, chair and all, he toppled forward, just as Hanson scrambled out of the way.

On his knees, he looked around wildly for Kelsey—and then grinned.

"Attaboy, Shorty!" he yelled.

Kelsey had run toward the back of the restaurant to escape through the alley door but Winters' wizened little cook was advancing from that direction brandishing a large meat cleaver. And Kelsey was backing away in front of him.

Walter Hanson went to meet them and Kelsey, caught between the cleaver and the gun, raised his hands sullenly.

"Marjorie," Hanson said, "will you phone the—"

But already there was the wail of a squad-car siren.

"Migosh," Shorty said, "they must have heard the ruckus all the way over to the station! What happened?"

Walter Hanson, sitting on a stool at the counter, with Burke on one side of him and Shorty, the cook, on the other, was still explaining that after the bodies had been taken away in the wagon. A bluecoat on duty at the door was keeping out the curious and explaining that the place was not open for business.

Burke took a swig of the coffee and winked at Marjorie.

"Reckon the war won't last long," he said, "once Wally here gets across and starts them commando tactics on the two-bit gangsters over the pond, huh?"

But Marjorie, surprisingly, didn't smile back. Her face went dead serious as she turned and asked:

"Walter, *are* you,. . . When?"

He looked up at her, almost afraid to believe that she was really interested; that interested.

"Not for a week yet," he said, "and then I'll be in a camp nearby for a while, and I'll get furloughs and—and—uh—"

Burke reached around behind Hanson and poked the cook.

"Gwan back and make me a pork chop sandwich, Dopey," he growled. "Know how to fry a pork chop?"

"Me?" Shorty said. "No."

"I'll show ya then," Burke said. "C'mon quick before this mug gets pitching woo. If he does that as sudden and violent as he starts riots, he'll need lots of room."

THIRTY CORPSES EVERY thursday

I

The palms of my hands were wet with sweat, and I wiped them on my whipcord breeches as I turned into the dark alley leading to the back door of the bus station.

I had no business driving this run, because I was scared stiff.

Probably the biggest reason for my not backing out was that it would have been too easy. I'd just left Baldy Weston, the local manager. He'd been just too damn sweet about it.

"Listen, Bill, I keep telling you that you don't have to take this Thursday run. I'd just as soon you didn't. Shorty Kline is going to deadhead the trip because his ma's sick in Los Angeles. He can just as well drive her through to the relief in Yuma. I put you up just because it was your turn and the rules give you the trip, but it'd save the company money if Shorty drove it. We'd have another seat to sell if we didn't deadhead him. So if that nutty idea's still in your head and you're the least bit squeamish about it—"

"Dammit, Baldy!" I'd almost yelled it at him. "I'm not trying to get out of driving her through. Shorty's a swell day man but

he's not good on night driving and you know it, and I got a better chance of not going off the edge of that roller coaster than
he. I want you to—"

"Yeah, yeah, you want me to re-route it over the regular run.
But we have reservations in Nadejo, through to L.A., and I'm
not going to phone there and tell them we're afraid to run our
bus down to get them. What we want is—"

"What you want is thirty corpses every Thursday!"

Baldy glowered at me, but I went on talking before he could
cut in. "Yeah, I know last Thursday missed, but how about the
two before that? Both busses full, too. Dammit, Baldy, we can't
go running busses into nowhere. Lord, look at the publicity we
had on those first two, two weeks in succession. We can't—"

"Then don't, Bill. If you want to drive it, keep her on the
road, that's all. That business about accidents running in
threes is pure superstition and you know it. Anyway, didn't Joe
get the same run last Thursday and take her through without
a scratch in the paint? Then why—?"

And that's where the bald-headed coot had me cold. I
didn't know why. Logically, there wasn't an earthly reason why
I was afraid to make that run.

The Thursday set-up is this. Our regular route, two busses
a day, goes through Globe and straight on to Phoenix. But
there's another way, south of Globe. That's Nadejo, and we
route one bus a week through that way, the Thursday night bus.
We get a few fares to and from Nadejo, but mostly it's to hold
a franchise that may be valuable some day.

And two Thursday nights in a row those busses had gone off
the road. Not in the same place, but in those mountains you
can't run off the road without dropping a hundred feet to half
a mile.

There had been no survivors of those wrecked thirty-pas-
senger sleeper coaches. The newspapers had played it up, of

course. But people go on riding busses just the same. And maybe I was wrong, because the bus last Thursday had gone through, just as Baldy Weston had pointed out.

* * *

But be that as it may, here came my bus from the other end of the alley, Woody Trenton at the wheel. A good mechanic, Woody. He swung it into the back driveway of the station, and I hurried up to be there when he stepped down. I'd had a talk with Woody too, that afternoon.

The door opened and he got out, grinning. "Running like a dream, Bill. And no water in the gas."

I put my hand on his arm. "Did you check—everything I told you to?"

He nodded soberly, and he looked so long into my face that I wondered if I showed how scared I was. "Yep, Bill, everything. Steering knuckle. King pins, tires, axles. And I done like you told me; I stayed right with the bus from that check on. Nobody came near it but me."

"Thanks, Woody. I—I guess maybe I'm being an old woman about this, but I can't think those others were—accidents. Lee Carey was the best driver we ever had. Nobody can tell me he just misjudged and went off into nowhere. And Sperry, too—"

He stepped back toward the alley, pulling out a pack of cigarettes. Employees aren't allowed to smoke in the station or on a bus. I followed him and took the cigarette he offered me, but I stood where I could keep an eye on the bus.

"Bill," he said, "I think you're hay-wire on this. They were accidents, couldn't have been anything else."

I nodded. "You're probably right," I told him, and wished I could believe it.

"Bill, don't think I didn't give Sperry's bus a real going over. Lee's accident had us all on our toes. And don't forget we had experts from the factory examine what was left of both of those busses. They couldn't find—" He broke off and shuddered a little, and I didn't blame him.

Woody shook himself, probably unconsciously trying to get rid of the pictures in his mind. "And don't forget, Bill, there was a witness to one of those accidents."

I nodded; of course I knew about that. Old Jess Bergstrom, a cattle buyer who sometimes drives himself to the coast and sometimes goes with us, saw Lee Carey's finish.

He'd driven that night because he'd started out too late for the bus. He'd caught up to the bus and was only fifty yards behind it when he saw it go over. He figured Lee had been going faster than he realized.

Woody flipped his still glowing cigarette in a gleaming arc down the alley. He said, "Jess is going with you tonight."

I looked at him open-mouthed for a minute. "You mean he's going, after seeing that other bus—"

"He went last Thursday," Woody drawled. "The old geezer has nerve, I guess."

For just a minute I was madder than hell. Was Woody razzing me, implying that I hadn't as much nerve as a guy like— Then I realized he wasn't. Nobody but me knew how scared I was about this trip.

I ground out my cigarette and walked back to the bus. We were due out in fifteen minutes. Mig was putting baggage in the compartment.

I strolled up to the ticket window "Good load?" I asked.

Ma Murdock, who sells tickets for us, nodded. "Twenty-five booked. Capacity, with the three pick-ups at Nadejo and with Shorty deadheading."

"All through as far as Yuma?" I asked, and she nodded.

Yuma's where the other driver takes over. I figured it quick. Twenty-five and three and Shorty and myself; thirty, once we got past Nadejo. A full load. And the other accidents had happened past Nadejo.

I got in the bus and took the tickets of the passengers who were already seated, and then sat down behind the wheel.

Shorty Kline came in. He looked different out of his uniform; I'd forgotten he wouldn't be wearing it on this trip. I booped the horn and he turned around and grinned and then came over to the window.

"Give me your hat, Shorty," I said. "I'll put it on the front seat to hold it for you, so we can chew the fat."

"Sure," he said, and handed it in.

Someone rapped on the door. I opened it and old Jess Bergstrom got on.

"Young feller," he said in a high squeaky voice, "you drive careful tonight. I saw that there other driver—"

"Yes, Mr. Bergstrom," I cut in. I didn't want to hear, just then, about what he'd seen, and it wasn't good for the other passengers to hear it either.

He glared at me a minute, annoyed at the way I'd cut him off, but I started the engine and pretended not to notice.

A few more got on and then Shorty came out of the station, the breeze making ripples in his blond hair, and while he was getting on I turned around and counted noses. All seats were filled but three.

II

I heard Mig, the Mex who acts as everything from baggage master to redcap, slam the baggage compartment. So there wasn't anything to wait for. I put my foot on the clutch and shoved the gear-shift lever into low.

Shorty said quietly, "Your lights, Bill."

I turned them on and said, "Thanks," rather shamefacedly.

"You feeling all right, Bill?" Shorty asked, and he leaned forward so none of the passengers could hear. "You don't look so hot."

"I feel okay, Shorty," I lied. My throat was kind of dry and my voice probably wasn't quite normal, but over the roar of the motor running in low and the meshing of the gears as I stepped it up, nobody would have noticed it.

Despite the fact that I had Shorty up there near me, I didn't feel like talking. We left the town behind, out on the open road which stretched for a while as straight as a die across the open desert. Then foothills, and soon we'd be in the mountains. Not such bad mountains, before Nadejo.

The road started gently upward, and the engine purred like a contented lion through the night. And what a night it was, for anyone in the mood to appreciate it.

The bus steered beautifully. Almost too easily for my mental comfort; I couldn't get my mind off what would happen if I turned that wheel too far just an inch or two. Once when we passed a wide truck coming the other way, I found I was gripping that wheel so tightly my fingers ached.

Then things levelled off and got easier for a short stretch, and I found I was lonesome. I said, "Swell night, isn't it, Shorty?" back over my shoulder and he said, "Sure, Bill, it's a darb."

He hunched forward so we could talk confidentially again, and said, "Bill, you sure you're feeling okay tonight? You don't look right to me."

For a minute I went hot and cold with sheer anger, and then I realized it was myself I was mad at and not Shorty, and I saw myself a lot better then, and knew why I'd insisted on driving the bus. And suddenly I realized it would do me good to get it out of my system. I pitched my voice so low.

"Shorty," I told him, "all that's wrong with me is that I'm scared stiff. That's why I wouldn't let Baldy take me off the run when he wouldn't reroute it. It's something I've *got* to lick, Shorty, see? If I gave in and let somebody else drive, I couldn't ever look myself in the face again."

"But listen, don't worry about me. I can drive just as well as if I wasn't scared. Better. I'll take this bus through on schedule, unless—"

"I see what you mean, Bill," he said slowly. "I—say, what do you mean by that 'unless'? Unless what?"

"Unless something happens that I haven't got anything to do with. Dammit, Shorty, I don't think those other two wrecks were accidents."

"Sure they were, Bill. Those busses were okay. Our men checked them, and the bus manufacturer's expert, and—hell, there was even an F.B.I. man looked at them."

"The devil there was! I hadn't heard about that, Shorty. Say, how come they sent for him if they—if somebody—didn't have a hunch there was something screwy?"

"They didn't send for him; he wasn't here about that at all. But he happened to be in town about the time of that second wreck and he went out there with the local sheriff. He was here looking for some bank robbers. The Welland National job."

I whistled softly. "Did they find the guys here?"

"Naw, he had what he thought was a lead, but it petered out. They ain't even got one of the four guys yet. And none of the money or securities turned up anywhere, either. Guess they're practically giving up hope of getting 'em."

The road was going up again, and I quit talking to keep all my attention on it. Funny I hadn't heard about that F.B.I. man being in town. Particularly on that Welland Bank business; it had been back East but it had made headlines all over the country; not because the hundred thousand dollars involved had been so large, but because it had been unusually bloody. Eight people had been killed in the getaway; three cops, two bank employees, and three bystanders.

On through the night, and now the road was getting dangerous. I kept all of my attention on negociating those curves —and staying alert for the unexpected; a car rocketing toward me taking more than its fair share of the road. Or—or what? A barrier of some sort, a boulder in the road? Hardly, because anything big enough to deflect a bus would have left a mark of some sort. And not only that, but one of those accidents had been seen,. . .

Accidents? There I was back again where I'd been.

Then an easy stretch again, and I was able to relax this time because we were due for a stop before Nadejo and the real roller coaster. I'd have a chance to get out for a cup of hot coffee and relax.

Pete Marks, who ran the little rest stop, wasn't very good at making sandwiches, but his coffee was swell.

Over my shoulder I said, "Hey, Shorty, we're almost to Pete's."

For a minute he didn't answer, and his voice came sleepily when he did. I guess he'd been dozing and I'd wakened him. He said fuzzily, "Huh? Who's Pete?"

I remembered then that Shorty probably hadn't made the Nadejo route for a few months, and wouldn't know Pete, who'd bought out the previous proprietor only three months ago. I explained, and Shorty just said,"Oh" and let it go at that, and a minute later I heard a gentle snore, and envied the guy. If I hadn't been so bull-headed about proving to myself that I wasn't yellow, Shorty'd be behind the wheel now and I'd be back in town tearing off sleep myself.

We slid into the driveway beside Pete's little place and I switched on the overhead lights and said quietly, "Rest stop.

Ten minutes." It was one o'clock and several of the passengers were sound asleep. Shorty, I noticed, was dozing. So was Jess Bergstrom, halfway back in the bus.

* * *

About a dozen people filed out and went into Pete's place. There were stools for only half of us, but that doesn't matter on a bus stop; people have been sitting down so long they're glad of a chance to stand up for a while.

I shepherded my flock through the door and followed them in. Pete Marks looked sleepy himself; Thursday is the only night he stays open this late, just to pick up our trade.

But he snapped into quick action dishing out sandwiches he'd got ready and opening bottles of coke and pouring coffee. A steaming cup of java, already creamed and sugared, was on the end of the counter, and Pete caught my eye and jerked his thumb toward it as I came in. He gave the drivers a jump on the passengers by having their java ready when he heard the bus coming.

I said, "Thanks, Pete," and leaned against the wall, sipping the coffee. It tasted swell.

Pete is fast; he had something in front of everybody within five minutes, and that gave them ten to eat or drink it. Sure, a ten minute rest stop always takes fifteen minutes; we say ten so the passengers hurry it up a bit. If we called it a fifteen minute stop, we'd have to allow twenty.

It's funny to watch a guy Pete's size working that fast on a job like that; he's six feet three and built in proportion and looks like he'd fit better in a boxing ring or something than behind a counter. And he's got bushy black hair that stands straight up on end and makes him look even taller, and light blue eyes.

He came across and leaned against the end of the counter,

and I was afraid he was going to say something about the accidents, and hoped he wouldn't because the passengers were crowded in so close to us they couldn't help listening.

"Nice night," he said. "Got a good load?"

I nodded. "Full up," I told him. "Or will be by the time we've passed Nadejo."

"Get much business out of there?"

"Not so much. Sometimes one or two, sometimes none. But nearly always through fares to L.A."

He said, "You must have quite a few getting on tonight, if this is all—but I guess a lot of 'em are asleep."

"Yeah," I told him. "Just three getting on at Nadejo. We got the rest. How's business?"

He shook his head mournfully. "Not so hot. Fewer people driving this route since—"

"Skip it," I cut in quickly.

He said, "Sure, I get it." He picked up another mug and filled it from the coffee urn and then put it down on the counter. "Better fuel up good," he said, "You look dopey tonight. This one'll cool down while you finish the first."

I said, "Thanks," and he went back along the counter and started collecting change from the passengers. Idly, I estimated the take; couldn't have been more than a buck and a half, and he'd stayed open at least a couple hours extra. In a way, I felt sorry for Pete; he couldn't be making any more than a living out of the place and it must be lonesome as the devil living way out here at the end of nowhere. The previous owner hadn't liked it. But then maybe Pete did; maybe he was a hermit by nature.

I put down the first mug empty, lighted a cigarette, and then picked up the second. There was a hair stuck to the side of the mug and I picked it off, thinking Pete was getting sloppy. I noticed something about that hair but it didn't register particularly just then. It was black, but it was light in color at the root.

Well, it had been on the outside of the cup, so it didn't matter, and I got rid of it down under the counter so no one would notice. The second mug was still too hot to drink but I got it cool enough to finish by the time the fifteen minutes were up.

Then I said, "Time's up, folks," and we went back to the bus. Shorty was snoring again. I gave him a gentle shove and he moved his head and quit snoring without waking up.

III

We rolled into Nadejo. It's a noisy little town, even at two o'clock in the morning. We haven't any station there, but the least villainous of the tavernkeepers sells tickets for us and phones us how many seats to hold.

I braked to a stop in front of his place. Three men—rather tough looking mugs, I thought—were waiting on the edge of the sidewalk. They had only one suitcase apiece, small enough to go inside, so I saw I wouldn't have to open up the luggage compartment.

I opened the door and they climbed in and gave me their tickets. I said, "I held three seats at the back for you. Okay?"

One of them said, "Yeah, we're together. Thanks, buddy." I switched on the ceiling lights, dimly, until they'd found the seats, then I slid the bus into gear again, and we rolled out of Nadejo. The moon was up now, a full moon.

This was where the road got mean. We were going up now, and pretty soon we'd be hitting the worst of it. You keep your eye on the edge of the road, and try not to think about that drop. And if you're nervous, you find you're gripping the wheel so tight that your knuckles are white and even the muscles in your shoulders ache.

And I was nervous, all right. I'd thought I'd managed to get all the scare out of my system, but I hadn't. We were getting into it now—and it was going to stay this way for a long time—and I felt worse. My head felt sort of empty and I had to keep blinking my eyes to keep them in focus.

I was tempted to wake Shorty and ask him if he'd take over, but I didn't dare. I didn't dare because I knew I'd be admitting to myself I was yellow, too yellow to drive this trip. I told myself that I *had* to go through with it.

Then I noticed something else. I wasn't driving the bus straight; despite my concentration on the wheel, I was weaving. One minute my wheels would be an even six feet from the edge of nowhere, and I'd intend to keep them on that imaginary line. The next minute they'd be only three feet, or two, from the edge, and I'd give the wheel a quick yank that would take me too far back the other way.

And it wasn't the steering mechanism of the bus. It was *me*.

I realized that suddenly, and I took my foot off the gas and put it on the brake instead—and I brought that bus to a slow stop.

And the minute it stood still and I could take my attention off the wheel, I realized that I was as sick as a dog. Not only my stomach, but all over. Fright didn't do this to a guy; I'd been poisoned. I was pretty sure I knew where.

I reached back and waked Shorty, shook him hard. I said, "Shorty! Snap out of it." He said, "Wha-what? What we stopped here for, Bill? What's up?"

I said, "Shorty, you got to take over. I can't drive; I'm sick. I—I think I'm poisoned."

I'd heard footsteps from the back of the bus, and looked up

and one of the three men who had got on at Nadejo was standing there. He asked sharply, "What's up?"

I said, "Everything's all right. We're changing drivers, that's all."

"Didn't I hear you say you were poisoned?" he wanted to know. He didn't look sympathetic about it, particularly. The dashboard light reflected in his eyes, and they were as hard as marbles.

Shorty was standing up by now. The guy who'd been talking turned around and began a quick whispered conference with the other two who'd joined him.

Shorty was saying to me, "But listen, Bill, if you got pto-maine or something, the first thing we got to think about is a doc. It's almost fifty miles to the next town where I know there's one. How far we out of Nadejo?"

"Six or eight miles," I said, "But you can't turn this bus around. There isn't a place you could for another ten miles, and by the time you came back that ten you might as well have gone on."

"But—" Shorty started to protest.

The foremost of the three Nadejo passengers had turned back to us. A couple of the other passengers must have caught part of the conversation, for I saw them getting up. I didn't want to start a panic, and I slid out from behind the wheel. "Sit down and drive, Shorty," I said. "We'll waste more time arguing than it'd take us to—"

"Say," said the Nadejo passenger. "There was a sort of siding only a few hundred yards back, and a flivver truck parked there, headed the way we came. There's a doc in Nadejo—"

Shorty looked at him. "Road-gang truck," he said, "But it'll be locked. How—"

"Hell, I can take care of the lock. I'm a locksmith."

Shorty said, "I can back—"

For some reason I felt a little better standing up than I had sitting down behind the wheel. I cut in: "I can walk a couple hundred yards, Shorty. I—I'm not so bad; it's just that I saw I wasn't fit to drive. Another mile and I'd have taken us off—"

Just beyond here had been the end of the line for Lee and Sperry. In their case, there hadn't happened to be another driver deadheading the trip. Had they been poisoned, too, and failed to recognize the fact as quickly as I had?

The Nadejo guy had hold of my arm. He said, "Listen, I want to get back there anyway. I've thought of something." He turned to Shorty; "I can get him back to the truck."

Shorty said, "Okay," a bit reluctantly, and then added, "and gee, thanks a lot."

One of the others of the Nadejo party was saying, "But listen, hadn't one of us ought to go with you?"

The one who had my arm said, "Naw, you wait for me in Yuma; fix a stopover there. I can take care of this." Somehow I had a hunch he wasn't talking about me.

We stepped down, the guy still holding tightly to my arm so I wouldn't pitch over the edge, and I found I could walk okay. Shorty yelled out, "So long, Bill."

The bus stood there until we had a good start, and I turned my head around and saw Shorty getting back in. He'd stood there in the road watching until he'd been sure I was walking all right.

We got to the parked truck, and I sat down on the running board while he climbed in and worked around under the dashboard. After a minute or two I heard the sound of the starter and then the engine began to turn over. He said, "Climb in, buddy," and I did.

By the way he drove you could tell that he wasn't used to driving on roads like those. He took it slow and easy down that steep dangerous part until we were almost in Nadejo; then he gave her the gun, and was still feeding it to her when we crossed the main drag.

We were almost out of town again before I realized that we'd probably passed the doctor's office. I said, "Hey, did you forget about—"

And by the time I'd got that far, we *were* the rest of the way out of town.

Out of the side of his mouth he said, "Forget the doc. You won't need one. We're goin' to see a guy about some poison."

"Huh? You mean Pete Marks?"

I saw him glance at me quickly. "Ain't so dumb, are you, pal?" he said, but there was nothing pleasant in his voice. "So you did dope it out who fixed you up. You'll go a long way, pal, if you live to do it."

My eyes were going off focus again, and I blinked them a couple times and got them clear enough for one good look at his face. It wasn't reassuring.

It gave me a faint ray of hope. I said, "Listen, if you're going to kill Pete, what good am I along? Let me try to walk back to—"

He said, "You're just exhibit A, pal. But you're right I don't need you. If it'd make you feel better, I can leave you here."

Something about the way he said it made me ask, "Alive?"

"No, pal, not alive."

IV

The pain was getting worse now; I was sitting almost doubled up with it. The man who'd just given my death sentence was bigger than I, and it was a million-to-one shot if I tried anything.

And we were quite a few miles beyond Nadejo now. I'd never have made it on foot, even if he'd let me off. My only chance would have been to catch a lift, and there wasn't much night traffic.

One idea—one slim chance—seemed to remain. If Pete Marks had poisoned that coffee, he'd know what poison he'd used. He might know the antidote; if it was something like raw eggs and milk he might have it. But I was going with a guy who was going to kill Pete Marks.

I didn't know I was thinking aloud until I'd said, "Pete Marks must be Bull Mahan!"

The car swerved a little, as though the guy at the wheel had jerked involuntarily. He barked, "How the hell did you dope that?"

Well, I'd said it, and it wouldn't hurt to talk some more. You can't be killed more than once. So I talked.

"Pete—I mean Bull—has his hair dyed. I happened to find that out tonight. He's blond. And Bull Mahan, who's six-feet-three and blond, is the only one of the Welland Bank robbers that was identified. And that leaves three of you, the three that got on at Nadejo. Four guys robbed the bank."

He chuckled. "You're a smart fellow. Go on; what's the rest?"

"Bull knew you three were at Nadejo, leaving for L.A. by bus. One bus a week, so—Say, I remember now he pumped me on how many reservations out of Nadejo. When I said three he gave me the second cup of coffee. If there hadn't been any, I wouldn't have got it; I mean it wouldn't have been poisoned. There weren't any passengers out of Nadejo last week, and that's why last week's bus got through. But why'd he want to kill you three?"

"Why'd you think?" he growled. "The double-cross, of course. Bull's a smart guy. So are we. We stashed that dough in L.A. and agreed not to touch it for six months. Three of us been hiding out in Nadejo, near the border. Bull'd been spotted, so he done different. He dyed his hair and—well, you know what he's been doing." I nodded.

"While ago," he went on, "we wrote Bull we weren't waiting

the full six months. There'd been a fed, we heard, snooping around Craigville, and that was kind of near. We told Bull we was going to L.A. to get the dough and we'd get his share to him or he could come along. We mentioned we'd go by bus."

I saw the whole vicious plot now, and it almost literally made my hair stand on end. For seventy-five thousand dollars—the difference between a one-fourth cut and all of the swag—Pete wanted to kill his three accomplices.

And he'd been willing to kill a whole bus-load of people, innocent people, to do it so it wouldn't look like murder!

Probably Mahan had thought that first bus-load would be all he'd have to tip over. Then, from the newspapers, he'd have found out that the passengers who got on at Nadejo weren't the ones he'd wanted. He tried again.

Those busses had been checked, and no one had thought of making autopsies on the drivers. Or had they? Maybe it was something that wouldn't show up in an autopsy unless the doctor who made it knew what to look for.

Sixty people killed, in an attempt to kill three! And it would have been ninety if I hadn't stopped that bus when I did. But why hadn't Lee and Sperry stopped?

For some reason I wasn't feeling any worse now. Maybe I was getting numb. Maybe it was the beginning of the end. I closed my eyes and tried to think what poison could have had just this combination of physical reactions, but I don't know anything much about poisons.

I got my eyes working again enough to figure out where we were; just a mile from our destination.

I glanced again at the face of the man behind the wheel; and I read death there. There was no mercy in those marble-like eyes. As soon as he'd killed Bull Mahan for double-crossing them, it'd be my turn. Or maybe sooner.

Maybe when he stopped the car, he'd get me out of the way before he went after Bull. He just hadn't taken time to do it yet. My purpose was accomplished, from his point of view. He'd offered to take me back just for an excuse to get out of the bus and go back without arousing suspicion. Of course, I'd be missed—or found—but he and his companions would be safe in Los Angeles by then.

Coming up was the turn and a hundred yards beyond the turn was the lunch-counter-filling-station.

The guy from Nadejo reached forward and turned off the ignition, and the engine went silent. He threw the car into neutral and I saw he was going to coast from here, so as not to take a chance on Bull being awake and hearing a car stop.

He held the wheel with his right hand and reached into his left coat-pocket. Obviously he was left-handed if he packed his gun there. It came out holding a heavy black automatic—by the barrel.

I didn't have to be a mind-reader to see what that meant. He wouldn't be going in after Bull Mahan with a clubbed pistol. It meant that the minute the car stopped, he was going to club me with that gun, before he went after Bull.

We were almost at the turn, now, still going thirty-five. I glanced out the side, trying to guess my chances on a jump. They didn't seem too good. I'd probably survive the jump, but he'd come after me with the gun held the other way.

There just wasn't any cover, anything at all in the flat landscape except the big spire rock that the turn in the road led around. And we were making that turn now, and I saw my only slim chance and didn't stop to think about it. I lurched across and jerked the wheel.

From some reserve I found the strength to do that, and at the same time to slide down into the seat, throw my free arm up to protect my face.

I felt the wheel wrench out of my fingers, and felt the jerk as he slammed his foot on the brake; but both were too late. We couldn't have been more than a few feet from the rock when the brakes took hold for we hit it with a crash that seemed like the end of the world.

The instrument panel seemed to have come back a couple of feet, and I was wedged in, but I pulled myself up free and turned to look at the Nadejo guy. I looked away again quick; he was dead.

I got out of the car—there wasn't any door left on my side. My legs wouldn't work and I sprawled flat. But I got hold of the car to brace myself and stood up, and then walked around to the other side. I found his gun.

From that side of the car, I could see Pete's place. It was darkened, but I saw the front door slam back and he came running out.

He must have recognized me, even at that distance, by my driver's uniform, for he ran toward me, holding a pistol.

I had an automatic in my hand—but I didn't want to use it unless I had to. The thought uppermost in my mind was an antidote for that poison he'd given me, before it was too late. I tried to run behind the truck, but instead I fell down on the running board.

I pushed myself up, but my feet didn't work the way I wanted them to. I lurched forward two steps away from the car and straight toward him. He was fifty feet away then, and my vision was so blurred that there seemed to be a quartet of black-haired shirt-sleeved giants running toward me.

Then the quartet stopped and raised four pistols and aimed them at me, but there was only one shot. It missed.

Without my seeming to have anything to do with it, the heavy automatic in my hand came up—pointing somewhere in his general direction—and my finger pulled the trigger. And the automatic began to explode in my hand, one shot after another.

Then the gun was silent, hot in my hand, and my fingers must have relaxed, because I heard it hit the road. And Bull Mahan, whom I'd known as Pete, was standing there swaying stupidly, even as I myself was probably swaying. His gun went down slowly, a last involuntary jerk of a muscle fired a shot that went into the road almost at his feet. Then his knees relaxed and he crumpled.

I was staggering toward him, and I made it on my feet half-way there, and on my hands and knees the rest of the way.

I shook him, yelling at him and using the name I'd known him by: "Pete! Pete! That poison—what is the antidote?" But I was shaking a corpse, and the distant yapping of a coyote was the only answer to my yelling.

The shack seemed miles away, but it was the only chance— to find a labeled bottle that would tell me what I wanted to know. I got about ten yards toward it, crawling, when somebody put out the moon and the stars.

* * *

Sunlight was streaming in a window when I woke up, and I was lying on a strange bed in what seemed to be a private room in a hospital. I felt lousy.

Obviously, someone had found me in time and everything had come out okay, but I started to thinking back and I felt lower than a mole's instep.

Then the door opened and a nurse came in, and she was a dazzler. Even through a stiff white uniform you could see she had a Dorothy Lamour figure, and she had red hair that looked like it was on fire when she crossed the shaft of sunlight from the window. And she had a face that looked like—if you can picture it—a madonna with a twinkle in her eye.

She said, "How are you feeling, Mr. Dineen?" I said, "Terrible. What happened? I mean, afterwards—if you know."

She smiled. "The papers are full of it. After you were found by a driver who brought you back to Craigville fast, the police here phoned Yuma to get the other driver's version. And with what he told them, they had the Yuma police get the other two men."

"What did Pete use on me? I mean what kind of poison?"

"Colitalis; one of the sulphanilamide derivatives. But it isn't a poison. It just affects co-ordination. The other two drivers didn't even feel it; didn't know they weren't co-ordinating right until too late. But it hit you quickly and violently because of your condition, and—"

"What you mean, because of my condition?" I demanded belligerently.

"The flu, of course. You had no business trying to drive at all that night. You should have been in bed then! Why, you were coming down with one of the worst cases of flu we've had in here in weeks; you've been out for—"

"The hell!" I said, and tried to sit up, but didn't quite make it. "Uh—pardon the language, but here I thought—"

She turned away to reach for a thermometer in a glass on the table, and shook the mercury down. "You've talked enough for now," she said, "and don't think too much either. You're here for a week, so you've got lots of time for both. Open your mouth."

She smiled at me again and she looked so darn beautiful that I said, "Lookit, you must have an evening or two off a week. Next week, will you—"

"The patient is showing the first sign of recovery. I'll put it on the chart. Open your mouth."

"But will you?"

She frowned and it made her look even prettier. "Certainly not, unless you behave yourself and open your mouth so I can take your temperature."

So I did, and maybe one fever sort of counteracted the other, because the themometer didn't break.

A MATTER OF death

The bus pulled into the union depot on Vine Street and the driver called out:

"Dinner stop, folks, half-hour."

I had to step out into the aisle to let the plumbing supplies salesman who'd been sitting next to the window get out. But then I sat back down again.

"I'm not hungry," I thought. "I'll sit this one out."

Cincinnati—I hate the town. The town I was never going back to.

Sure and I was back there now, but if I didn't get off the bus it didn't count. I leaned back in the seat and tilted my hat over my eyes.

And everything would have been all right if it hadn't been for that glass of beer I'd had at the last rest stop. If it hadn't been for that one glass of beer, I'd have made it. One glass of beer.

The humor of it didn't strike me until I was on my way back to the bus from the wash-room.

"You're in Cincinnati, Jack," I told myself. "You got off the bus, so you're in Cincinnati again. And drinking did it. Drink made you leave this town six years ago, and now—solely because of one glass of beer—you're back here again.

"Then don't be so grim about it. It's childish to go back and sit in that bus, like a kid with the sulks. You're twenty-eight now, and you're not a kid any more."

So I went through the waiting room and stood on the sidewalk of Vine Street, and I was home again.

It looked just the same. It looked like Vine Street always looked at five forty-five in the evening. Some of the stores had different signs on them and there was a haberdashery across the street where the cigar store used to be, but everything in general looked pretty much the same. The same yellow street cars with the same familiar names. Colerain. College Hill. Spring Grove.

"I wonder if Charlie's place is still around the corner," I thought. "There's time for a beer."

It was still there, but Charlie wasn't behind the bar. I asked, and was told he came on about seven o'clock.

"That's good," I thought. "Then you won't see him. At seven you'll be an hour's ride to the east. You'll get through here without seeing a soul you know. You won't have to talk to any of them. Let them keep on thinking you're dead, or whatever they do think."

So I sipped my beer slowly and when I looked up at the clock, it was a quarter after six, and the bus was gone. And I knew then that I'd intended, all along, to stop over for the night.

I knew that I wanted to see some of the people I didn't want to see at all.

It occurred to me I'd better get myself a hotel room while

there were still some open. I walked two blocks north to the Clinton and registered for a two-dollar room.

A little pudgy man in shell-rimmed glasses who was sitting in the lobby looked at me curiously as I walked past him. As though he knew me. But I'd never seen him before. I was pretty sure of that.

It occurred to me as I signed the register that I should have bought a change of linen on my way there, so I could bathe and change. You get pretty dirty riding on a bus, and my suitcase was on its way east ahead of me.

I told them I wouldn't go up to my room just yet, and went out to look for a men's furnishings store that would still be open. As I crossed the lobby I saw the pudgy little man get up and stroll toward the desk. Probably, I thought, he'd mistaken me for someone else and would find out his mistake when he read my name on the register.

I found a store, finally, and bought what I needed. But I'd walked back past Charlie's place searching, and it was seven-fifteen when I started past it again, back toward the Clinton. Charlie would be behind the bar now, so I stopped in. The bath could wait a few minutes.

He was behind the bar and I walked up and stuck out my hand. He looked at me a minute before he took it. Something was wrong with the way he looked at me and something was wrong with the way he shook my hand.

"Hello, Jack," he said.

"Six years, Charlie," I said. "I've been gone six years and you say hello like I'd been gone six hours."

He grinned, but it wasn't a whole-hearted grin. It was— well, it looked wary, cautious.

"Back for good?" he asked, and looked relieved when I said I'd be gone by tomorrow noon.

"Where's all the gang?" I wanted to know.

"In the Army, a lot of them. Most of the rest are around. Some of 'em will be in later. You look—a little not so good, Jack. Still hitting the bottle too hard?"

I laughed. "Hit one too hard this afternoon. That's why I stopped here overnight. If I hadn't—"

A customer down at the other end of the counter rapped a coin on the wood.

"Stick around a minute," Charlie said, and went down to take the order.

Something was wrong. "Stick around a minute," from Charlie. Guys don't change that much in six years.

"I shouldn't have stopped over," I thought. "I hate this town. I'll always hate it."

I'd have got off the stool and walked out, but I didn't want to act childish. I waited until Charlie came back. I asked for a beer and he drew it.

"What's been happening," I asked.

He started to say something, hesitated.

"You know that your father—uh—"

"Died five years ago," I said. "Yes, I heard it. A month too late for me to come back. I was in Mexico then." I thought a minute and then said, "I wish I'd heard it sooner and been closer. I'd have come back, even if it wouldn't have done any good. I mean, he wouldn't have known it. I wish—"

I didn't go on with it, because I didn't want to sound mushy. What I really wished was that I'd come back during that *first* year, before Dad had died, and squared myself with him. He'd been pretty much right in kicking me out. I'd been a pretty dissolute young pup.

But it was too late to think about that now.

"Your uncle, Ray Stillwell," Charlie said. "You heard he's married?"

I shook my head.

"Three years ago."

"Good," I thought. "Uncle Ray's a good guy. I hope he got the right woman."

Charlie must have been a mind reader.

"Crazy about her," he said. "A society gal, but not one of the stuck-up ones. They drop in once in a long while. They get along."

"Good," I said.

There was a silence. I hadn't asked the question I wanted to ask. I mean, about Margie.

Six years is a long time. But I found out then how badly I wanted to know.

"Charlie," I said, "have you seen—"

And then the guy at the other end of the bar rapped his coin again. I didn't want a quick yes-or-no answer so I said:

"Go ahead, Charlie. I'll ask when you get back."

I sipped at my beer. Six years is a long time. "You shouldn't ask," I thought. "You've forgotten. You've got over it. Let it go. You don't really want to know."

I heard the outer door opening and turned around.

It would have been the devil of a coincidence—if it had been a coincidence.

She came in with a fellow who looked familiar to me, but it took me a few seconds to place him. His name was Gerald Breese and he was a clerk in the law office of John Garry, who had been my Dad's attorney.

But I hardly noticed him. I was looking at Margie Delaney.

Six years wasn't so long. At first I thought she looked just the same, and then I saw that there were changes, and that they were all for the better. She was more beautiful, more poised and mature. She wasn't a pretty girl—she was a beautiful woman now.

"Margie," I said, and she turned and saw me. Her eyes went wide and there was a sudden flush of color in her face.

She opened her mouth to speak, and then Breese had stepped in between us. He said something to Margie that I couldn't hear, but his voice sounded urgent, insistent. Margie hesitated, then she turned and walked out.

Walked out without having spoken to me at all.

Gerald Breese turned, then, to me and cursed me. Quietly. No one else in the place could have heard him.

I think that if he'd said anything even less than that, I'd have killed him. His stepping in between Margie and me had been enough.

But that was too much. For some reason, instead of intensifying the sudden red mist of anger, it drove it away. It left me sitting there not angry at all, but cold and hard and curious.

Something, I knew, was more than met the eye. Charlie hadn't been cordial, exactly. Margie had cut me. And now this bozo whom I barely remembered, . . .

I let go of my glass of beer on the bar and put my hands in my pockets. They'd be safer there, I thought.

Breese's face went pale and he stepped back quickly. It took me a second to realize he had thought I was going for a gun.

That tore it. I laughed, and turned away from him, back to the bar. He stood there a minute—I could see him in the mirror—then turned and went out.

Charlie came back.

"You were going to ask—" he said.

"Never mind," I told him

He had been busy down at the other end and maybe he hadn't seen what happened.

"You don't look so good, Jack," he said. "Maybe you've had too much already. Shall I fix you a mountain oyster?"

And then again, maybe he had seen what happened. A bartender generally glances toward the door when it opens, even if he's mixing a drink.

Anyway, I realized suddenly that I wasn't enjoying Charlie's place, or his company. I told him I didn't want the mountain oyster and I got up and walked out.

I should have waited a little longer. Margie and Breese were talking just outside. Margie looked angry and so did Breese. I turned the other way so I wouldn't have to go past them, and I walked rapidly.

It was dark now.

I found myself looking into the window of a novelty shop on Fountain Square. It was full of bright practical jokes to play on people. Artificial bugs. Exploding matches. A cushion that miaouwed when sat upon.

"I hate this town," I thought.

I should have stayed on the bus. I shouldn't have stopped over. I should never have drunk that glass of beer which was the cause of my getting off the bus.

II

I walked back to the Clinton. I said "Six-fourteen" to the clerk behind the desk. He turned and started to reach for the key. Then he turned back.

"Oh, six-fourteen," he said. "You're Mr. Trent. A friend of yours has been waiting for you to return and he borrowed the key so he could wait in your room. Mr. Zimmerman."

"Lovely," I said. "Who is Mr. Zimmerman?"

He looked surprised. "You mean you don't know him? But he said it would be all right and showed me his card. And I knew you hadn't been up to your room as yet and could have left nothing there, and—uh—I'm sorry if I shouldn't have let him up."

"What did the card he showed you say, besides Zimmerman?"

"Cincinnati *Herald*. Uh—I think the first name was Walter. Yes, Walter Zimmerman, Cincinnati *Herald*. But—uh—from the way he spoke, I gathered that he was a friend of yours, not that he wanted to see you as a reporter."

I had to laugh at that. You don't expect naivete in a hotel clerk. But this one looked pretty young. He'd probably been at the job all of a week or two.

I told him it was all right, and I rode the elevator up to the sixth floor.

The hallways at the Clinton are well-carpeted. I had no reason for trying to walk silently, but my footsteps along the corridor didn't make much noise.

Because, just as I reached out my hand for the knob of Six-fourteen, I heard a voice say:

"Lajoie?"

Were there two men in my room?

"Zimmerman calling, Lajoie," the voice went on, and I realized then that he was talking over the phone. Not loudly, but the transom was wide open and I could hear distinctly. I stood there without moving.

"Yeah, I'm onto something that may be big, but I want you to know where I am, just in case, . . . No, I don't know in case what. Maybe in case the guy throws me out the window when he finds out what I've got on him, . . . Yeah, Jack Trent. Took Room Six-fourteen at the Clinton and I'm waiting for him. Yeah, in his room. Look up the morgue on him and have it ready. Yeah, might be a big story. I can't tell till I talk to him. Jerry says he's a killer, and, . . . No, don't send cops over. He's not wanted that I know of, . . . Sure, you might check with Headquarters. Just say you heard a rumor he's back in town, but don't tip our hand. I want an exclusive, . . . No, I won't take any chances. I'll just ask him why he—"

The clang and rattle of the elevator door drowned out the rest of that sentence and two elderly women got off the elevator and turned down the corridor toward me.

I couldn't just stand there listening. I had to go on into the room or move on, quick.

I moved on. I didn't want to go in till I'd had time to sort out in my mind what I'd just heard. Zimmerman was waiting for me and wouldn't run off.

So I walked on. Toward, I realized, the blank end of the corridor. But a door at my right said "Shower" and I turned in there.

I bolted the door and leaned against it to think.

Not that it did any good. Something was rotten in the State of Ohio—that far I could get, but no farther.

It just didn't make sense. Five minutes later it still didn't and I realized that I might just as well have gone into Six-fourteen right away instead of stalling.

So I went out into the hall and down to Six-fourteen and this time I opened the door and walked in.

The room was empty.

The light was on and the key was inside the door, but the room was empty.

"Lovely," I thought. "He's maybe hiding in the closet to surprise me. After telling the clerk he'd be waiting here and leaving the light on, the key in the door, he wants to surprise me."

Sure it was a screwy thought, but everything that had happened since I got off the bus had been screwy.

I went over and opened the closet door, and I was right, dead right.

He surprised me.

He surprised me by falling out of the closet with a thud that seemed to shake the whole hotel. He was as dead as a salted mackerel, and he hadn't got into that closet and died of heart failure waiting for me. There was blood matted in his hair. That meant he hadn't committed suicide, either, because suicides don't generally hit themselves over the head.

He had been murdered.

I sat down on the bed for a moment, and then I got up and rolled him over for a better look.

He didn't look any better rolled over.

It was the pudgy little man who had looked at me curiously when I'd walked through the lobby an hour or two ago to register. He still wore the shell-rimmed glasses and neither being murdered nor falling out of a closet had knocked them off.

I took his wallet out of his pocket and looked at the cards in it. A press pass made out to Walter B. Zimmerman, Cincinnati *Herald*. Other identification to match, and twenty-two dollars in bills. I put the wallet back in his pocket.

"Lovely," I thought. "Oh, lovely."

Because it wasn't just finding a corpse in my room. It was an air-tight frame for murder. Motive—Lajoie would prove a motive after that phone call he had just heard from Zimmerman, who had said he was waiting for me and "had something" on me.

Had Zimmerman actually made that phone call and then been murdered? Or had he been dead then, and had I stood outside my own door listening to the murderer frame me? Well, the frame was just as tight in either case.

I got up and walked to the window and stood looking out, thinking.

The hotel clerk's evidence. Lajoie's evidence. Oh, it was beautiful. Perfect.

I could call the police right now, wait for them to come, and go to jail with them when they left, to await my trial.

Or I could blow town.

Or I could get myself in deeper.

I decided to get myself in deeper. I turned out the light and left my room.

I tossed my key on the desk and scowled at the clerk.

"Nobody was in my room," I told the clerk, "but the key was in the door. Fine system. Did you see him go by the desk on his way out?"

"Why no, but, . . . Well, I might not have noticed him if I'd been talking to another guest or, . . . I was back in the washroom once for a few minutes, but—"

"Haven't been in the hotel business long, have you, sonny?"

"N-no. But I wouldn't have given him your key, Mr. Trent, if you'd been up to your room at all or had a chance to leave any of your property there. But as you hadn't, I thought—"

"Okay," I said. "No harm done, but don't do it again."

I left him slightly flustered and apologetic, which was what I wanted to accomplish. If I'd walked out alone, without bawling him out, he might have started wondering what had happened to my guest, and might have sent a bell-boy up to investigate. But now I'd spiked his guns and given him something else to worry about. I'd given myself time before the body would be found.

And, of course, tightened the noose around my own neck.

I went over to Central Avenue, where the hock shops grow. I bought myself a pistol. I didn't know yet what I was going to do with it, but its weight in my pocket was slightly comforting.

I went to the *Herald* office, and leaned against the information desk to talk to the little blonde who turned around from the switchboard to ask what she could do for me.

"Zimmerman in?" I asked.

She shook her head. "Day shift."

"Doesn't he ever drop in evenings?"

"He'd have come by here. I'd have seen him."

"Oh," I said. "Then you know him by sight. I'm not quite
sure he's the guy I want anyway. Is he about five feet five, sort
of pudgy, wears shell-rimmed glasses, black hair?"

"That's him, yes. Anyone else you'd want to talk to?"

"Who's in charge of the editorial room now?"

"Mr. Lajoie. Night city editor."

"N-no," I said. "That isn't the name. Who's city ed, days?"

"Mr. Monahan."

"That's the guy. I remember now. Well, I'll drop in tomorrow and see either him or Zimmerman. Thanks, sister."

Not so good, I thought. If the corpse in my room had been
a phony, it might have been something to work on. But he was
a bona fide newshawk, and Lajoie was a real person, too. A city
editor, whose testimony would do me no good.

Maybe, I thought, I should kill Lajoie. And the hotel clerk.
And the elevator operator. And dump the corpse out the window and let the police guess which floor it came from.

And burn down the hotel so my name wouldn't be on the
register.

And failing that, I thought, maybe the next best thing would
be to see Charlie again. And this time make him open up as to
what made the cool breeze across the bar.

I headed for Charlie's place. I just might get something to
start on.

I wasn't expecting anything pleasant, and that's where I got
fooled again. The minute I stepped in the door.

Margie Delaney, sitting alone in a booth, had been watching
the door. She came up to me.

"Jack," she said, "I'm sorry. I didn't mean to be rude. I—"

"It's all right, Margie," I said. "Let's sit down."

I led her back to the booth and sat across from her. There weren't many people in the place and the booths on either side were empty, so it would be a good place to talk.

"Gerald told me to go outside and wait—that it was important," she said. "I thought he was going to bring you out with him. Then he came out alone and—we quarreled. I left him and came back in to see you, but you were gone. I waited here, hoping you'd come back. I didn't know any other way to find you."

"And I did come back," I said. "So everything's all right."

"Everything's all right," she said. Her hand, on the table, moved nearer, and I put mine over it.

"Everything's all right," I thought. "Everything except a little matter of a murder rap."

"I came back here," I said aloud, "to ask Charlie some questions. But maybe I won't have to. Maybe you know the answers. What happened here since I left?"

"Why, what do you mean?"

"I mean that when I came in here tonight I didn't get a rousing welcome, even from Charlie. And your friend Breese—he wasn't exactly enthusiastic about renewing our slight acquaintance. Has somebody been telling tales out of school about me since I've been gone? Or what?"

Her eyes dropped. She didn't pull her hand back, but I took mine off it. I didn't want any sentiment mixed in with this. I wanted it cold.

"Weren't you arrested for killing a man in New Orleans two years ago?"

"Go on," I said.

"And released for lack of evidence? And there was a man

here who said he knew you in El Paso, and, . . . Well, were the things he said about you true?"

"Such as?"

"That you were a puller-in, whatever that is, for a gambling place there and—and had other jobs like that, but couldn't hold them because you were drinking too heavily again. And, . . . Oh, other stories of that sort."

"Where did you meet this gentleman from El Paso?" I asked.

"In here, one night. I stopped in alone on my way home from working late, and he was talking to Charlie. I heard most of what he said."

"Had he been to New Orleans, too?"

"No, that was in the newspaper. It—it wasn't a big story, but somebody showed it in here. A little reporter from the *Herald* showed it to Charlie and asked if it was the Jack Trent who used to come here. Of course, it might not have been."

"Jack Trent's a common name," I said. "Was the reporter named Zimmerman?"

"I believe that was his name. Charlie said it must be some other Jack Trent. But then when the man from El Paso—"

"I see," I said. "Anything else?"

"It seems trivial beside the other things, but you didn't come back when your father was dying. His attorney, Mr. Garry, wrote you three weeks before your father actually died. He had an address then in El Paso, and the letter never came back, so you must have got it. Or did you?"

"I got it," I told her.

III

Margie and I were silent a moment. She hadn't moved her hand, and I put mine back upon it.

"I got the letter," I said, "three weeks too late. I was working for a mining company deep in Mexico then, and our mail

came in by burro, once a month. In the same mail was a newspaper three weeks old, with an account of Dad's death."

Her hand turned, under mine, palm upward and her fingers
gripped mine.

"I knew it must have been something like that," she said.

"I had a good job with the mining company," I went on. "I
stayed there until the radio got excited one Sunday in Decem-
ber. Took me two weeks to get back and enlist. I was in Australia
when some guy named Jack Trent got in trouble in New Orleans. And I was on Makin Island about the time the gentleman from El Paso was here in Cincinnati. I got a medical dis-
charge a month ago and was heading—"

"Jack, were you wounded?"

"Only by a mosquito. I'll be completely okay in six months
or so, and I'm going to re-enlist then if they'll take me back.
That is, if it looks then like they'll still need me."

"Jack, I'm so glad! Then *none* of it was true! I don't understand about the man from El Paso. You've explained about the
letter Mr. Garry sent, and it must have been another Jack Trent
in New Orleans, but this man from El Paso said it was *you.*
Charlie showed him that snapshot of you and him the time the
two of you went hunting up on the Little Miami River and he
said yes that was the Trent he'd known in El Paso. It must have
been a deliberate lie. But why?"

"I don't know," I told her.

"But, . . . oh, it doesn't matter now. You're back, and everything's all right."

Her hand tightened on mine. And that reminded me.
Everything was not all right. There was the little matter of a
murder.

"Margie, listen—" I said.

And then I realized I couldn't tell her. Not without making
her an accessory after the fact, if the case against me held.

"Wait a minute, Margie," I said, and went to the telephone booth back at the end of the room.

I couldn't remember the first name of Garry, the lawyer who had handled my father's affairs, but I remembered he lived in Walnut Hills and found his phone number.

I called it, and he was home. I told him who I was, then asked:

"How much of an estate did my father leave?"

"It'll be about eighty thousand, after all fees and taxes."

"Will be?" I said. "Why the future tense? Mean it hasn't been settled yet?"

"No. I've been trying to get in touch with you, Trent. It's rather a complicated situation."

"He disinherited me, didn't he? I understood Uncle Ray was to get the estate."

"Well—yes and no. Where are you calling from?"

I told him.

"Can you come out here to my place this evening?" he wanted to know.

I hesitated. "Maybe. But can't you tell me, roughly anyway, what it's all about? Now, over the phone."

"Well—"

"Look, then," I said. "Can you possibly grab a taxi and come down here? Someone's with me, and I'd rather not leave now."

"All right. I'll be down in twenty minutes."

I stepped out of the phone booth, and the first thing I noticed was that the other customers besides myself and Margie— there had been three or four of them—were gone.

Charlie was just closing the outer door. He walked back to me and stuck out his hand.

"Margie just told me, Jack," he said. "Forgive me?"

"Sure." I shook his hand and almost got the bones of mine crushed. Charlie has a grip.

"Jack, I should have known those stories were phonies. I don't know why I gave them a thought."

"Skip it," I told them. "I don't blame you."

"Look," he said. "The place is yours tonight. I shooed out the riff-raff, and the drinks are all on the house for you and everybody you want to invite down. It's a welcome-home party for the rest of the night."

Somehow, *now*, in the jam that I was in, that hurt worse than the cold shoulder I'd got from everybody earlier in the evening.

"Thanks, Charlie," I said. "Thanks a thundering lot, but I'm afraid it's not my night to howl."

"What do you mean?"

I saw I had to tell at least part of it.

"Come on and sit down," I said.

I sat next to Margie and Charlie sat across from us. And I talked, wording it as carefully as I could. When I'd finished, they knew what the score was, but they didn't know anything specific enough to make them accessories.

"You should have called copper, Jack, the minute you found him," Charlie said. "You'd've been cleared."

"Would I? Don't forget that call he—or the guy who killed him—made to Lajoie at the *Herald*."

"It would have looked black. But you made it look blacker. Gosh, what a mess!"

There was a minute's silence, then Margie said:

"That man who said he was from El Paso, Jack. He might be a lead."

"I never saw him before or after," Charlie said. "But lemme describe him to you."

"Let me try," I said. "Middle-aged and just beginning to show it, but he'd been good-looking once. Wore good clothes, well-kept, but a long way from new. Maybe even a patch or two, but his shoes were shined and he was freshly shaved. Looked and talked more like New York than El Paso. Good voice, but slightly overdramatized everything he said."

"You know him, then?" Charlie cut in.

I shook my head. "Guessing. Giving you a sketch of an actor out of work. The kind of out-of-work actor who'd slipped just far enough he could be hired to pull a con like that. For twenty bucks."

Charlie nodded slowly. "Now I think of it, he probably was an actor. Listen, Lajoie was here that night."

"He comes here?"

"Sure. He and Zimmerman. And your—"

Somebody tried the doorknob, then rapped on the glass. Charlie went to the door and it was Garry, the lawyer, so he opened up and then locked the door again when Garry had come in.

I sat him down with the rest of us.

"I—I really shouldn't give you this information for six more days, Trent," he said. "But six days isn't much out of five years and such minor matters were left to my discretion as executor. In fact, your father told me that—"

I'd glanced at the calendar the minute he mentioned six days and I interrupted.

"You mean, Mr. Garry, that in six days Dad will have been dead exactly five years?"

"Yes. As you know, he made a will completely disinheriting you. But after you'd left, he made another will. It provided that, after specific bequests, the bulk of his estate was to go into a trust fund for five years. At the end of five years, you were to receive it, under certain conditions. The conditions were that you had—ah—shall we say, reformed?—ah—found yourself, overcome your youthful wayward tendencies and—ah—"

"And what?" I demanded.

He coughed deprecatingly. "And kept out of jail. Your father felt it deeply that time seven years ago when you were arrested for disorderly conduct and for resisting an officer. About that point the will is specific and incontestable. If you have been in jail, on any charge, you forfeit the inheritance. Ah—have you been?"

I shook my head.

I was beginning to see light, although I didn't yet see where it came from.

"I haven't been," I said. "But there are six days to go?"

"Yes, six days. And of course, if you are wanted by police authorities anywhere—or, to be technical, if you are wanted six days from now, you would also forfeit the inheritance. But that, of course, is unimportant."

"Of course," I agreed.

"Because certainly, now that you know the conditions of the will, you will take no chances for the short time remaining. But—ah—you can prove your whereabouts during the time you have been gone? Of course, it will be my duty, as executor, to check up. There have been rumors which have led me to believe, until now, that the check-up would be superfluous, that if we *did* find you, you would not even claim the estate under the will."

"Ask him the sixty-four-dollar question, Jack," Charlie said.

I realized then that I'd been stalling on doing just that.

"Who inherits if I do go to jail?" I asked.

"Your uncle, Mr. Stillwell."

"The devil you say," said Charlie, and saved me saying it.

The light had gone out, the light I'd begun to see when I heard the terms of that will. Because Uncle Ray was a swell guy. He couldn't want money badly enough to frame a murder charge on me to get it. Let alone commit a murder himself to do it.

Not that Ray Stillwell didn't have his wild moments. But murder wasn't in him

Charlie stood up. "Just the same," he said, "I'm going to get him down here. Might as well make it a party."

I didn't object and Charlie went back to the phone booth. He came back and said:

"He was working late at his office. Union Trust Building. He'll be here in a few minutes. He's blame glad to know you're back."

And Uncle Ray was glad. I could tell that by the way he shook hands when he came in a few minutes later. But he looked different. He had aged plenty in the six years since I'd last seen him. There were lines in his face that hadn't been there before, and crows-feet of worry around his eyes. He wasn't dapper any more, either.

There was something wrong, but not in the way he greeted me.

Charlie had gone over behind the bar. Now he came back with a freshly-opened bottle of White Horse, some soda and a tray of glasses, and put them on the table.

It should have been a party, but it was a wake.

I could tell by Garry's manner and Uncle Ray's that they could feel something was wrong.

There wasn't any use holding out, but I didn't want to have to do the telling. And I wanted, suddenly, some fresh air and to be alone for just a minute.

"Charlie, tell them," I said, "I'll be back in a minute."

I went to the front door and stepped outside, throwing the catch so I could get in again. I stood there a minute and then I turned and looked through the glass at the four of them, inside. Charlie talking. Margie. Uncle Ray. Garry.

"They're swell people," I thought.

Why did I hate this town, just because I made a fool of myself here once, a long time ago when I wasn't much more than a kid? They were real people, and so were all the other friends I had here. It was I who was wrong, not the town.

Does one always find out things too late, I wondered.

And then it was Margie alone I was looking at, and I realized that there again was something I'd found out maybe too late.

I didn't want to go in again until I saw Charlie was through talking, and I turned around to face the street again, leaning back against the door.

"All right," I told myself, "you were so smart, and now what? You were going to clear yourself. You still haven't the faintest idea who killed Zimmerman."

The sudden squeal of hastily-applied brakes made me look up. A car had stopped suddenly in the middle of the street. There was a big man in it. I thought I recognized him but I wasn't sure.

He swung the car into the curb, got out and came back, walking fast until he saw that I wasn't moving, then he slowed down. Yes, it was Moran. He had been a beat copper six years ago. Now he was out of harness, but he was still a cop. You could tell that just by looking at him.

"Hello, Moran," I said. "They find Zimmerman?"

He nodded. "There's a pick-up order out for you. Sorry, Jack, but I'll have to take you in."

"I'll go," I told him. "I'll go, but I didn't do it. I didn't kill him."

"I wouldn't know about that," he said. "But I hope you're right. I wasn't on the case. I don't know what they've got on you."

"Plenty," I told him. I tried to laugh, but it didn't quite jell. "The only hope I see is that there may be too much," I said. "Look, I've got friends inside here. I'll have to tell 'em I'm going."

IV

When I walked back through the door, Moran came right behind me. There was a dead silence from the group in Charlie's.

"A wake," I thought. "It's really like a wake."

I tried to speak lightly. "A little matter has come up. I'm going down to Headquarters with Moran. Be gone only a few minutes."

It didn't go over.

"Sure, Jack," Charlie said. He came over and put his hand on Moran's arm. "Listen, Irish," he said, "I want to talk to you. Come on over by the bar."

"Won't do any good, Charlie," I told him. "Moran's not on the case—don't know anything about it except the pick-up order."

"Just the same," said Charlie, "I want at least one copper to have your side of it. Won't hurt you to have a friend down there."

"I'm already Jack's friend," Moran said. "But I gotta take him in."

Charlie propelled him to the bar. "Then we'll have a drink on that, and you'll listen. He won't run away and there's no hurry."

I was almost sorry Charlie had done that. Now I'd have to face the others again. I didn't want to look at Margie. So instead I turned to Garry, the lawyer.

"May I ask you a question, sir?"

"Of course, my boy."

"Who, besides my uncle, would benefit by my going to jail? Benefit financially, I mean."

"Why, no one."

"Not even you?"

"Not even me." He smiled wryly. "In fact, I'd probably be better off the other way, a little. For if you should inherit, I could at least hope you'd let me continue management of the estate. Your uncle's a lawyer and a C.P.A. himself. He won't need me. And for the same reason—"

"Yes," I prompted.

"That's on the assumption, which happens to be truth, that I've managed the estate honestly. If I hadn't, my motive for wanting you to inherit would be even stronger. You can see that."

"Sure," I said glumly, "I can see that." Obviously, he could fool me to cover up any irregularities, a thousand times easier than my uncle.

A blank wall. Nothing but blank walls.

I strolled over to the bar, wishing Charlie and Moran would hurry up and get it over with. Then I thought of something I'd wanted to ask Charlie.

"Charlie," I said, "who—besides this Lajoie—might Zimmerman have called to tell I was in town? He must have called someone *before* he called Lajoie. Someone had to know he was there waiting for me, in order to go there and kill him."

Charlie shrugged. "Dunno. Jerry, maybe. Zimmerman and Lajoie and Jerry hung out together a lot and were all pretty close. And he knew Jerry knew you and might have phoned him to tell him you were back."

Jerry! That phone call I'd overheard. I'd forgotten. "Jerry says he's a killer."

"Who the devil is Jerry," I asked.

"Why, you know him. Gerald Breese."

Gerald Breese, I thought. Gerald Breese! The guy who had cursed me at thirty-two minutes after seven o'clock. Who had come in here with Margie, maybe because he's heard from

Zimmerman I was in town, and knew where to find me.

But there wasn't any motive, *any* reason!

Then I turned around again and saw my uncle's face. It was dead-white and had that shocked look I'd seen on the faces of men who have been hit by a bullet in a vital spot, whose minds know they're dead before their bodies find it out.

I saw that he knew the answer now, and that gave it to me.

It was an answer I didn't want, because it meant that to make a case against Gerald Breese, Uncle Ray would have to be ruined, somehow. Uncle Ray, recently married to a woman he loved deeply and who loved him.

"Jack," he was saying in a curiously flat voice, "I'd better tell you that—"

"Shut up," I said.

I whirled back to Moran. "Listen, Irish," I said, "I know who killed Zimmerman. Breese did. I know why, and how. But it would be the devil and all to prove."

"So?" Moran said. "Well, give us the dope and we'll try. I'll try. But first I got to take you down to Headquarters."

"No," I said. "You'll never prove it, then. Neither can I, after tonight. But you let me talk to Breese now, right now, while the iron is hot and, . . . Well, if it doesn't work, then we go down to the station and that's that."

"But, man, I can't wait," Moran said.

Charlie put a hand on his shoulder. "Listen, Irish—" he said.

"All right, all right," Moran said. "But I got to go along."

I nodded. "Just so he doesn't know you're along. He's got to think I'm alone."

"Why?"

"It's bluff, all bluff. Maybe it's a wild idea, but I think I may put it over. Come on! What are we waiting for?"

And then we were getting into Moran's car. Charlie and Margie and Uncle Ray were getting into the back seat, over my protests and Moran's.

"Shut up," Charlie said, slamming the back door of the sedan. "This is a party, ain't it? You can't kick us out yet."

Charlie directed us to the apartment building where Breese lived.

"First floor back," he said. "And there's a light on. He's there."

"Good," I said. "The ground floor's a break. Moran, you got skeleton keys?"

"Sure, but I don't know about using them."

"I'll go in the front way, back the hall to his door and knock. He'll let me in. You go to the back, take off your shoes and let yourself in the back way. Just come to the door of the front room, and listen."

"Me go around to the back? How do I know you won't lam?"

"You don't," I said.

"All right, all right. I'm a sucker."

I got out of the car and went into the front door of the apartment building. I took my time walking the length of the hallway, to think out just what I was going to say, and to give Moran time to get around to the back.

I knocked on the door.

It started to open, and I lunged through it. With my left hand I shoved Gerald Breese back across the room, and with my right I yanked out the gun I'd bought on Central Avenue and aimed it at him. I kicked the door shut behind me.

"I'm going to kill you, Breese," I said.

I heard a faint noise from the back of the apartment and knew Moran was coming in. Breese didn't hear it. All his attention was on me and the gun aimed at the middle button of his shirt.

I tried my best to look desperate and kill-crazy. From the way Breese stared back at me across the room, it went over. He was scared stiff. He licked his lips.

"Trent, what's the idea?" he said. "I'm sorry I said what I did to you in Charlie's, but, . . . Lord, that's nothing to kill a man for, if he'll apologize."

"The devil with that," I said. "I'm talking about framing me for Zimmerman's murder."

"You're crazy! I mean, why would I do that?"

"For money," I said. "You've been blackmailing my uncle. You've got something on him. I don't know what, and don't want to know. But you've not only been bleeding him, you've figured to cash in big when he inherited that estate.

"And you meant to see he got it. You planted rumors about me, even hired an actor to spread them. But tonight when I checked in at the Clinton your reporter pal happened to be in the lobby and recognized me. He knew you worked for the firm that handled Dad's estate and phoned you the news. That's why you pulled that stunt at Charlie's."

He licked his lips again. "I don't see why I'd do that."

"It was a first feeble attempt. You got Margie and brought her around to Charlie's, and used her and then that clever little remark of yours to try to get me to attack you. You wanted me to go to jail on an assault charge before I could find out what it was all about." I laughed. "If it hadn't been so blasted obvious you *wanted* me to slug you, I would have. You overplayed. And the whole stunt was childish.

"You saw me start off away from the Clinton, so you went there, with a better idea. You knew, from Zimmerman's call, he'd be waiting in my room. Bump him off there, and let me take a real rap. I don't know whether you got him, at the point of a gun, to make that call to Lajoie and then killed him, or whether you killed him first and made that call yourself, impersonating him. I don't give a hoot which it was."

"That's silly, Trent. Curse it, you can't—"

"Can't prove it? No. I know I can't. I'm framed tight. That's why I'm going to make this a little personal matter. I'm going to lam, but first, I'm cashing you in."

I clamped my lips tight, like a man who's through talking. I raised the gun higher and sighted along the barrel. He was looking right into the muzzle. I started to tense my finger on the trigger.

"Wait!"

He almost yelled it. He was chalky white now. He had his hand out in front of him as if to ward off the bullet.

"Wait," he yelled. "Don't! Listen!" His voice was hoarse with fear. "I'll cut you in. Don't shoot me, and I'll make it worth your while. Ten thousand—"

"Nuts," I said. "I should wait around for it? Do I look as crazy as that?"

"I've got it! I've got ten thousand, out of what I've already got from your uncle. It's all the cash I got, but now I can get more. Look, you said yourself the frame is air-tight, so you've got to lam out anyway. But with ten grand you could go a long way."

I let the gun waver just a little.

"Okay, but first," I said, and took a step toward him. The toe of my shoe caught the edge of the rug and I fell like a ton of bricks.

The pistol flew out of my hand and slid across the rug, right to his feet. He stooped to pick it up.

He was straightening up with it in his hand when Moran yelled from the doorway:

"Hey, drop that!"

Breese whirled around. He must have realized, in that second, how he had been trapped. He must have been desperate. Because he whirled with the gun pointing toward Moran and his finger was tightening on the trigger when Moran's Police Positive cut him down.

I got up slowly. I felt weak.

Moran, his shoes in one hand and the pistol still in the other, was glaring at me. Coming up behind him, as though they'd been in the room but farther from the doorway, were Charlie and Margie and my uncle.

"You fool!" Moran said. "You didn't tell me you had a gun."

"You didn't ask," I reminded him.

"And then you practically throw it at him! Of all the dumb—"

"Dumb, your grandmother," I said. "That was beautifully timed and executed. I fell on purpose. Don't you see?"

"See what?"

"I had to play it that way, so you'd have to shoot him to take him. Otherwise, at a trial, he'd have spilled whatever he had on Uncle Ray. If I'd've killed him, it would have been murder, but if you shot him for resisting arrest that was something else again."

Moran looked stunned. "But, you dope," he said, "what if I hadn't been quick enough on my draw? What if he'd shot first?"

I grinned at him. "The gun not only didn't have bullets, but there wasn't even a firing pin. That's the only reason the guy on Central Avenue would sell it to me without a permit."

"So you made a sap outa me, then, just to put your trick over."

Charlie put a hand on Moran's shoulder.

"Listen, Irish—" he said.

Moran started to laugh, and I knew everything was all right.

More than all right, for I saw the look that was on my uncle's face.

And the look on Margie's.

Everything was going to be better than all right.

A FINE NIGHT FOR murder

It was a warm, delightful spring evening. Officer Sweeny strutted rather than walked along his beat, and twirled his nightstick nonchalantly on its leathern thong.

Why, he wondered, didn't something happen? Peace and quiet were well enough, but once in a while the weather made a man—even a big beefy-faced lug like him—feel romantic and adventurous. But of course it was Monday, and Monday's an off night.

He turned on to Dean Street, tried the door of the butcher shop on the corner and found that it was locked as it should be.

The next store was the restaurant. Mary Burke, the waitress, was looking out the window, as she always seemed to be looking out the window when she wasn't working. She caught Officer Sweeny's eye and smiled at him.

Officer Sweeny, softened by spring, sighed even as he smiled back at her. Lord, if he were only twenty years younger, he'd make a special point of finding out why a colleen like Mary Burke was serving meals to many men instead of cooking meals for one.

He pushed open the door and stepped inside. "Ah, mavour-neen," he said, "'Tis a night straight from the Emerald Isle. A night for the little folk to be out. Seen you any?"

Then he saw the Greek grinning at him, and Sweeny dropped the brogue. "Hullo, Dmitros. All quiet on the gas-tro-nomic front?"

"All too quiet," said the Greek. "No business," and his hands said it as eloquently as his lips. "Monday—she's an off night."

Sweeny nodded judiciously. "Yeah, Monday she's an off night. Well, Dmitros, don't take any lumberjack." He turned to go.

"Lumberjack? What is it, lumberjack?"

Sweeny grinned. "Wooden nickels, Dmitros. Wooden nickels."

He went out and closed the door gently behind him. But even as he closed it, he caught the liquid melody of Mary's laugh, and the evening was warmer and sweeter for the sound of it.

There was a car parked at the curb a few doors beyond, and sitting in the car, behind the wheel, was a man whom Officer Sweeny distrusted at sight. The man was looking across the street, and Sweeny followed his glance.

"Just out of jail, that one," said Sweeny to himself. And because he'd got himself thinking in the brogue, "'Tis the pallor of the dungeon upon him." Sweeny decided to stop and question him, and then discretion overcame thought, and he walked on. After all, he had no reason to question the man, and it was just a guess that he was fresh from jail. And whistling a tuneless, little melody, Officer Sweeny strolled on down Dean Street, . . .

Sitting there in the car, Walter Meers had seen the policeman turn the corner, step into the restaurant and out again. The officer was new to this beat, Walter knew; that is, he was new in the five years that Walter had been—away. His eyes went back to the house across the street, when the officer had gone on, and again he counted to make sure, so he could find it from the back.

His hand gripped the automatic in his pocket. For five years he had waited to do this thing. And now—when his rear vision mirror showed him that the policeman had vanished out of sight down the street, he got out of the car.

He walked past the restaurant without looking in—or he might have seen Mary Burke waiting on a customer who had just come in—and he crossed the street at the corner.

Half a block on he turned into the alley. Five houses down, and there was the garage. The car doors were closed, and it was empty. He went through the yard to the smaller door on the side nearest the house. A minute's work with a piece of stiff wire let him in that door.

He pulled it shut and stood there just inside the door until his eyes became accustomed to the darkness of the garage.

Then, when he could see a bit, he picked the place to wait for Delaney.

When the Donald Duck comedy had ended, Jim Delaney leaned over to the small figure in the seat beside him. He whispered, "We got to go now, son."

"But daddy, can't I stay and see—"

"Shhh. No. We've seen the whole show once, and I let you stay for Donald Duck twice, and it's late and goops like you should be in bed long ago. It's after eight."

"But daddy, can't we see—"

Jim Delaney grinned, but he stood up and reached down for Bobby Delaney. Bobby saw the reach coming, and was out of his seat in time.

Out in the lobby, Bobby asked, "Can I have some candy now?"

"No." And the boy almost had to run to keep up with Jim's. long strides. "Listen, goop, it's after eight o'clock and your— Mrs. Evans is going to tell me off for keeping you out past bed-time."

And a few minutes later, outside the theater, Jim Delaney was slightly appalled to see just how dark it was, and how late it was. Almost nine o'clock.

"Daddy, I'm tired. Want to go to sleep."

"Almost to the car, son. We'll be home in fifteen minutes and you'll be in bed in twenty."

"Can I ride in the back seat? Then I can curl up and go to sleep there?"

"Sure, goop."

"And can I sleep there all night, out in the car's house?"

Jim grunted. "We'll see about that. In you go, goop."

He looked back over his shoulder when he'd driven only a block, and Bobby really was asleep back there.

Yes, he would get a piece of Mrs. Evans' mind for keeping Bobby out this late. But he could put up with that; it was good to have a housekeeper who took enough of an interest in the boy to care what happened to him.

Not as good, of course, as having a real—

His lips tightened to a thin line. There was—*Mary.*

And now, a few months ago, she'd taken a job in that little restaurant right across the street. It couldn't be accidental, in a city this size that she'd happened to get a job right across the street.

A green light ahead of him flashed amber and he stopped suddenly. So suddenly that he looked back quickly to make sure Bobby was all right.

After that, he drove more carefully, and a few minutes later turned into the alley, . . .

Tenseness came into Walter Meers' body as he heard the car

slow down in the alley outside, and when he heard its door open and close he backed tightly against the wall.

The doors swung open, outward. Then he heard Delaney get back into the car and maneuver it into position for backing in. And then the rear end of the car was inching past him.

The car came on in, and stopped, and the lights went off. He could see Delaney in the car, but Delaney hadn't seen him yet.

Delaney got out of the other side of the car and came around front and closed and bolted the doors from the inside, still without seeing him.

Walter Meers stepped toward him then, his foot scraped along the concrete floor.

There was a momentary silence, a complete silence. Then, "Who's there?" There was no fright in Delaney's voice, damn him.

Meers moved closer, and when Delaney turned as though he was going to throw the doors of the garage open again, he said, "Don't do that."

Delaney said, "My money's in the inside pocket of my coat, if that's what you want."

It was more pleasant now, Walter Meers thought, to hold the trigger for a while. Once he pulled it, it would be over with.

He said, "I can use some of your money, Jim. You'll never miss it."

There was an almost inaudible sound from the other man. He said quietly, "You know me. Who are you? I can't place your voice."

Walter chuckled. "It's been a long time, pal. But maybe you'll remember when I tell you, you took Mary away from me. I kind of hoped she'd be in the car with you."

"Mary—Good Lord, you must be Walter Meers. You don't know that—Mary and I were divorced three years ago?"

"*You're lying! Damn you!*"

Meers almost yelled it, and his fingers were tense on the trigger. Damn it, the guy *had* to be lying or this didn't make sense.

Or did it? He'd stolen Meers' girl, hadn't he, and nobody could do that and keep on living. No matter what happened afterwards. The fact was—he'd stolen Meers' girl.

In jail, time went by and nothing changed and you didn't realize that things could change in the world outside. He'd been waiting trial. When he'd learned that Mary, *his girl*, was going to marry this Jim Delaney that he knew slightly. And later, just after he'd been sentenced, that the marriage had come off.

And he'd decided then, and stuck to it through five years of bitterness, of brooding. But this upset things for a moment, until it came to his warped mind that this made it worse. To have stolen his, Meers' girl—and then thrown her over?

He almost yelled, "You can't get out of it that way, you—"

Jim Delaney's restraining gesture was almost automatic. He said, "Shhh. You'll wake—"

And then, because he hadn't meant to mention the kid, he stopped. Suppose this crackpot jail-warped Meers knew *whose kid*—

"You *were* lying!" There was a sudden elation in the killer's voice. "She's asleep in the car, huh? I knew damn well that you were lying!"

And at the thought of it, of seeing her and having her in his power as Delaney was, Meers took a sudden stride toward the side door of the car.

Jim Delaney grabbed his arm to stop him. He said, "Stay away from there. It's just—"

But then Meers' other arm, the one with the gun, swung round at him. Blind rage and fear in the killer's mind, when he had felt that grip on his arm, didn't stop him from thinking, "*If*

I shoot, I'll have to run because of the noise. And I can't take time to kill her too, if she's in there—"

So the gun, as a bludgeon, swung at Jim Delaney's head. He jerked back, but not far enough. The flat side of the automatic's barrel thudded against his forehead. Delaney went down.

Walter Meers yanked the door of the car open. At first he could see nothing inside. He reached in and flicked on the dome light.

"The hell," he muttered. A kid. Would it be Mary's kid asleep there?

Could be Mary's kid.

He flicked off the dome light of the car and turned on the headlights instead. They'd show him whether another wallop was needed to finish off Delaney. He'd have to finish him or Delaney would squawk to the cops. He went around in front of the car, and bent over, putting his hand to Delaney's chest. Heart still beating.

Meers raised the automatic to deal the finishing blow.

Then he heard footsteps in the alley, heavy footsteps. Sounded like a cop's walk. Slowly and very quietly, he lowered the gun and crouched there against the double doors.

He wished now he hadn't turned on the headlights—but it was too late to change that. He gripped the automatic, ready to shoot, and waited, . . .

In the dimness of the alley, Officer Sweeny walked leisurely, with the air of a man enjoying a stroll. *What* a night it was. In winter and foul weather, he had often cursed the city fathers for begrudging a brighter light than the one way down at the intersection of the alleys.

On most nights, he disliked this detour that had to be made because on the opposite street there were two jewelry shops and a furrier. Checking the back doors of those places was more important than trying the front.

He'd passed the jewelry shops already, and now he tried the door of the furrier's. It was locked, as it should be.

Across the alley and a few doors down there was dim light within a garage. It would be—he counted the houses to make sure—the garage of Jim Delaney. Nice young chap, Jim Delaney.

If Jim was working in the garage, 'twould be well to pass the time of evening with him. He strolled across to the garage doors and peered in one of the panes.

Too bad, Jim wasn't there. The garage light itself wasn't on, as it would be if he were working on the car. Just the headlights of the car were burning.

Maybe Jim had forgotten them and he'd better go in and turn them off. He put his hand on the door handle, but it was bolted from the inside.

Should he go up to the house? Um—no. Probably Jim had left those lights on purposely because his battery was overcharged. Or maybe he'd left them on because he was coming back to the garage later.

A matter of small moment. He peered in again and rattled the door, just to make sure no one was in there. Then he strolled on, . . .

Walter Meers waited until those heavy footsteps had completely died away before he moved. A bad moment, when the copper had tried the door. But his luck was holding. He hadn't had to burn a copper down. It's bad luck to burn a copper.

He looked down at the unconcious form of Delaney. Lying there on his back with the red welt on his forehead where the gun had struck. But still alive, breathing. Damn the guy. Why hadn't he died. Then he could just leave him there, like that, and it looked sure as hell as though Delaney had fallen there, hitting his head on the bumper of the car as he fell.

It would be safer that way—for there'd be no hunt for a killer. And the breath of the law felt hot on Walter Meers' neck just at that moment, with the narrow squeak of the copper almost walking in.

He wondered, could he hit again on that same spot, harder but so squarely there'd be only one wound? Maybe, but wait! There was a better way, a surer way.

Just start the engine of the car, and leave, with all the doors and windows shut, and let good old monoxide do the job.

He stood up, and examined the position of the body critically, as a policeman would. Yes, it was quite natural that he might have fallen just so.

It was the work of a moment to start the motor of the car turning over—and luck was with him that it was a quiet motor and the copper who'd looked in wouldn't be sure it hadn't been running then.

He backed toward the door, and then hesitated as he remembered the kid in the back seat of the car. This was going to kill the kid, too. But he couldn't pull the kid out without botching the setup, the perfect setup.

To hell with the kid, let him die. *Mary's and Delaney's* kid, and the hell with it.

He let himself out the door, and locked it again with the stiff wire. Everything was now as it should be if Delaney had driven into the garage, got out before he stopped the engine, closed the front doors, then fallen as he started to walk back to the car.

No chance for slip-up now, unless Delaney came to before the monoxide did its job. And he'd take care of that. Back halfway between the garage and the house was a tree, and under it was black shadow.

He went back and leaned against the tree, safe there from

sight at any angle. Hand on the automatic in his pocket, he watched the garage. If Delaney tried to leave,. . .

Back in the garage, Jim Delaney was awake. He had heard the soft scuff of feet as Meers had gone to the door, and he had heard the closing of the door and the scrape of the wire in the lock. He had heard these things as something in a dream, without realizing what the sounds were, and what they meant.

When he opened his eyes, the headlights of the car blinded him, but he caught hold of the bumper and then the radiator and pulled himself up. And leaning against the car for support, he worked his way around it to the open window of the back seat.

And he could hear there the sound of Bobby's peaceful breathing, and the kid was all right. For a moment, he had feared—

And then, and only then, it came to him that the engine of the car was running. He had shut it off before he got out, he was sure. And now it was running again!

Suddenly and with awful clarity, he saw the plan of double murder. He leaned through the window of the car, reaching for the ignition key.

But before his hand touched it, he hesitated, and then didn't.

Suppose the murderer was waiting outside, to make sure. Of course, that is just what he would do.

Walter Meers couldn't take a chance now, now that he had revealed his identity and his intentions. For his own skin, Meers wouldn't *dare* go away and merely hope that his plan worked. From Meers' point of view, he, Jim Delaney, *had* to die.

And Meers had a gun.

It took will power to keep his hand off that ignition key, with the deadly monoxide coming out of the exhaust pipe back there— but he steeled himself with the thought that there would be no danger for five or ten minutes yet, at least.

Meers had just left, not over two minutes ago, and he wouldn't have stayed in the garage after he'd started the motor.

What was out there? How could he fool Meers into thinking his plan had worked, so he'd go away? And still save Bobby's life, and his?

He couldn't open a door or window without it being heard or seen from the outside—and he didn't know on which side of the garage Meers would be waiting. How then—?

Of course! The hose! That would do it.

Sitting on the running board, he slipped off his shoes before he crawled, keeping down out of sight as much as he could, to where the hose was. And he reached up over the workbench and found a roll of friction tape that he always kept handy.

He crawled back of the car, and was glad he had thought to bring the tape. The hose was a bit too small to slip over the exhaust pipe, but he butted them together and sealed the connection airtight with layer after layer of the black sticky tape.

It was dark back of the car, and the hose connection wouldn't show. And he ran the hose itself carefully around the wall and along the bottom edge of the front door, wedging the nozzle end in the crack where the two big doors met at the bottom. The gas was safely routed now, out into the open air of the alley.

One thing more, before he lay down again in front of the headlights. He found a wrench, a heavy wrench, and put it within easy reach of his hand but out of sight from the windows. If Meers *should* enter to make utterly sure his victims were dead, that would still give him a fighting chance.

Then he lay down in front of the car, and closed his eyes.

He had no way of keeping track of time, but he guessed—

and it was a rather close guess—that half an hour had elapsed when he heard footsteps walking around the garage. Furtive footsteps.

They paused at the side window, and from that window Jim Delaney knew he would be in full view. He lay very still and hoped that he had remembered the position in which he had been lying well enough to pass the test.

Then he heard the footsteps going away. This time he kept careful track of time by counting off the seconds. He wouldn't move a muscle until he'd counted off ten full minutes that way. Or better make it fifteen to be sure, . . .

Walter Meers knew that he had made completely sure, now. He'd even leaned his ear against the pane of that side window, and he could hear the motor of the car still running, just as he had left it.

By now, they were both dead in there. Both dead, and he was completely safe because Delaney could never tell anybody what had happened.

And he'd had to kill a kid he hadn't even known existed. Funny; everything was all mixed up. Maybe he'd been silly to come here at all. Dammit, probably if he met Mary now he wouldn't even want her. There were lots of women. Why, if he saw Mary now—

He went through the yard, straight to Dean Street where he had left the car. All he had to do now was get the hell away without being seen, or attracting any attention to himself.

He was halfway across the street, he happened to look at the restaurant, and for an instant he thought he *was* stir crazy and seeing things. For there, in a waitress' uniform, was Mary. Mary Burke, or Mary Delaney—looking at him so intently that he knew for sure that she recognized him.

It didn't make sense. Why would Mary be working in a restaurant *there*? Was she or was she not still married?

A car honked at him, and he jumped out of its way. Then he smiled and waved at Mary Burke and changed his direction to take him to the restaurant instead of the car he had left parked.

Regardless of what she was doing there and why she was a waitress, there was only one thing he could do now. Now that she'd seen him leaving a house where two people—one of whom he had motive to kill—would be found dead in the morning.

And he'd just been thinking—if I saw Mary now!

Well, he was seeing her. And she was seeing him, and that meant she could put a rope around his neck.

He walked into the restaurant, and smiled down at her—his best boyish, charming smile. He said, "Hello, Mary."

She was really a swell-looking kid, he thought. Even prettier than he'd remembered her to be. Too damn bad he'd have to kill her. Too damn bad.

Mary Burke had been surprised to see Walter, almost as surprised as he had been to see her, although she didn't know that.

Still wondering what he had been doing over at Jim's house, she said, "Hello, Walter. It's—it's been a long time, hasn't it? You've—" She wanted to say that he was looking better, but couldn't bring herself to lie that baldly.

He said, "What are *you* doing, Mary? I thought that you and Jim—"

"Didn't you know, Walter? I'm—I'm not married any more. But you must know that—you just came from Jim's. He must have told you."

That gave him his cue; he knew now. He said quickly. "Of course I knew. I wanted to see Delaney to ask him if he knew where you were, but he wasn't home. I wanted to see you again, Mary."

Mary Burke looked at him, puzzled by something in his manner. Something she couldn't quite put her finger on.

The Greek was strolling forward from the back of the restaurant, and Walter said quickly, so quickly that the words almost ran together, but softly so the Greek couldn't hear, "If you introduce me say my name is George Rawlings. I changed it since I got out, to give me a fresh start, see?"

By the time Mary had said, "I understand, Walter," Dmitros was near enough, and she introduced them, giving Dmitros the name Walter had asked her to give.

Walter said, "Glad to meet you," and then turned back to Mary. "What time are you through work? I've got a lot to talk to you about."

Mary said, "In a few minutes Wa—George. I'm through at ten."

The Greek smiled at her. "An old friend of yours, Mary?"

She nodded, and the Greek said, "Run along now. Ten minutes, what difference? Nothing to do anyhow."

Mary Burke went back through the kitchen to the little cubby-hole that she used for dressing, and changed into the organdie dress she'd worn to work.

When she came back, Dmitros was getting ready to close up for the night. Walter took her arm and led her outside and down to the car.

Mary hesitated before she got in. Somehow, she hadn't expected him to be driving. She asked, "Where are we going, Walter? I—I must be home early and—"

He smiled at her. "And you're afraid I might be annoying, huh? But that isn't what I wanted to talk to you about. Don't worry."

"But where are we going?"

"A quiet place I know of, where we can talk. You needn't be afraid of me, Mary."

There was something wistful about his voice. And Mary Burke decided that her vague fears were groundless, and got into the car.

****

Jim Delaney waited until he had counted from one to sixty, at a rate he knew to be pretty close to one number a second, ten times. And during those ten minutes, he hadn't heard a sound outside, although he'd listened with every nerve of his body.

Then he got up and went to the door, the small one that led into the yard. He unlocked it with his key and stepped through, tensed for a shot.

But there wasn't a shot, nor any sound save the street noises. To make sure, he ran around to the alley side of the garage and still all was clear. Then, and only then, did he go back and lift the boy out of the car.

Bobby stirred and opened his eyes.

"'Lo, Daddy. We home a'ready?"

Jim smiled down at him. "Yes, goop, home already." He cut the switch.

His eyes anxiously studied the boy's face for any sign of ill effect from monoxide, but there seemed to be none. He carried the boy up to the house and in at the back door.

Mrs. Evans, the housekeeper, was reading a magazine in the living room, and her lips were a thin line.

"Mr. Delaney, you *shouldn't* have kept that child out until—" Then she saw the bruise on Jim's forehead, and her face changed.

He spoke quickly. "Something happened, Mrs. Evans. I haven't time to explain; I've got to go to the police right away. I'll take Bobby upstairs for you; you can undress him there."

He carried Bobby up the flight of steps and into a bedroom. He put him on the bed.

Jim said, "He had a whiff of carbon monoxide. He's all right, but phone for Doc Burns to come across the street and look at him, soon as you get his clothes off. I'll be back—"

He ran down the stairs and out to the garage again, disconnected the hose, and got in the car. Best thing to do was drive right down to the station and tell them. Better than phoning.

He swung the car out of the alley, and then rounded the corner into Dean Street.

Across the way, a few doors from the restaurant, a car was just starting up, coming toward him. *Walter Meers was driving the car and Mary was with him.*

Jim Delaney was too surprised to yell or do anything for the second until they were past him. And neither of them had seen him; he was almost sure of that. He slammed on the brakes, jerked the gearshift viciously into reverse and backed to turn around. It seemed to take him minutes to maneuver that turn.

But when he had the car headed the right way, there was a tail-light in sight two blocks ahead that could be—that *must* be them. No car had passed him while he was turning, and unless Meers had turned off Dean Street and another car had turned on, it *had* to be them.

He stepped on the gas pedal to overtake the car ahead.

What was *Mary* doing in that car? Meers couldn't have known where Mary was or what she was doing—and that meant he'd met Mary for the first time *just* now.

Delaney's mind seemed to be racing as fast as the motor of the car, for he saw at once the implications of that meeting. The murderer—for Meers still thought he had murdered tonight—left the scene of his crime by walking between the

houses toward Dean Street. And Mary, working in the restaurant across the way, probably just coming off duty, saw him.

Meers was going to kill her. He wouldn't leave her alive
when she knew that he had been leaving the Delaney house at
just the time two people had died.

The gas pedal was down flat on the floor, and he'd gained a
block on the car ahead now. Still too far away to see it clearly.

Oak Street, a heavy-traffic street with stop-and-go lights,
was coming up ahead. The car he was following got through,
and the light changed against Jim Delaney.

And he had to stop—not because this was a time to worry
about traffic regulations, but because he couldn't drive through
or over a stream of traffic going against him. He edged his way
into it, impatiently. Brakes squeaked, and he got through
against the light.

But the car ahead had gained blocks. Grimly, Jim pushed
the gas pedal to the floor boards again. If a cruising squad car
had seen him go through the light back there, or saw him
speeding now, and followed, that would be swell. He wished all
the squad cars in town were after him. But in the rear-vision
mirror he could see that the street behind him was clear.

The car ahead—still three blocks ahead—turned into the
Wentworth Road. Jim swung his car at the turn almost without
slowing down. Almost, not quite, he turned over. But he'd
gained ground, and he knew he could catch them now. For
now they were out of the heavy traffic area at the fringe of town
and again, as they had been at the start, only two blocks ahead
of him.

Recklessly, relentlessly, he shortened that distance until he
was right behind them. And at a point where the road was
clear and straight ahead, he swung out to pass.

Once almost past them, he could edge his car to the side of
the road and—

Then he was up alongside them, and he shot a quick sideward look at the other car.

There were three people in it, all utter strangers.

Somewhere back there, either at the very start or when he'd been stopped at Oak Street, he'd lost Meers and Mary, and he'd been chasing the wrong car,. . .

****

Officer Sweeny sighed and turned into the alley behind Dean Street. His conscience had been bothering him, very slightly, for half an hour now.

Just because he hadn't investigated why Jim Delaney's headlights had been on, with the car in the garage.

Of course it was all right that they were, he told himself for the hundredth time. But there was a million-to-one chance that it wasn't all right. Suppose something had happened to Delaney in the garage?

And while he was back here, he might just as well try the doors of the jewelry shops and the furrier's place. He tried them, and they were all right, and then he reached the Delaney garage.

The big doors stood open and the car was gone. Of course. Delaney had been going out again, and he hadn't bothered to turn off the headlights; probably his battery was overcharged and he wanted to tone it down.

Yes, he'd been a sap to let it worry him. Officer Sweeny shrugged and strolled on.

It was a beautiful night all right, but he rather wished something would happen. Not much, but something. He was getting just a little bored.

****

Walter Meers guided Mary Burke around the clump of trees. He said, "There's a bench there at the top of the bluff. And you can see out over the lake. It's swell."

They were there now, and Mary drew in her breath a little and said, "It—it *is* beautiful, Walter. But isn't this the place where you—"

"This is the place Slim fell off the bluff. But don't tell me you think like the coppers did, that *I* pushed him off."

There was faint irony in his tone, but the girl didn't seem to notice it. She said, "They didn't ever say you pushed him, exactly, did they, Walter? Just that you and he had a fight up here, and—"

"That's what they said. But we didn't have a fight. He just— Oh skip it."

He could, he knew, tell her the truth and it wouldn't matter because she wasn't going to leave here alive. But there wasn't any hurry about that.

It wasn't as though he really wanted to kill her, or he'd do it right away and get it over with. He just had to, and that was different. He strolled forward to the edge of the bluff and looked down the steep slope toward the railroad tracks below that ran along the edge of the lake. He remembered how Slim had looked cartwheeling down that slope.

But that was because Slim had been off balance. A man could walk down it easy, if he wasn't pushed. He could even walk down it carrying a body.

And that's what he was going to have to do tonight. For this was a good place to kill Mary Burke, but a very bad place to leave her. The police would find out his connection with Mary

Burke, and they'd know what had happened to Slim Johnson here, and they'd put two and two together and pull him in.

But Mary Burke wouldn't be found here. She'd be found maybe hundreds of miles away.

That was going to be easy, because the freight trains went by slowly down there, pulling up the grade from the city. All he'd have to do was wait till a long one started by, then take her down there and push her body into the first empty boxcar that went by. Or even toss her over the edge of a gondola; she was light enough for that.

And the body would turn up in some town a hundred miles away, without identification.

Mary had sat on the bench, and he sauntered back and stood looking down at her.

She asked, "Walter, what was it you wanted to tell me?" And he knew from the tone of her voice what she thought it was and that she was trying to bring it into the open so she could put him in his place.

He smiled. "Let's talk about you first, Mary. How long have you been working in that Dean Street greasy spoon?"

"About four months. Before that I worked in a restaurant downtown."

"And it was accidental that you got a job where you did?"

She was twisting her fingers in her lap. "N-no. I—I had to find a way to be able to see Bobby, once in a while, as often as I could."

Walter sat down on the bench beside her. He made his voice sympathetic. "What happened between you and Jim, Mary?"

She didn't answer at first, and her voice sounded strange when it came. "I—oh, I suppose I may as well tell you, Walter. Maybe it will do me good to talk about it. Jim is a good guy, a wonderful one, Walter. Except his temper, and that isn't as bad as mine. We were awful fools, then. I think maybe we got married too young."

"But what happened?"

"We quarreled—over nothing, really, at first. And we got in with the wrong crowd and once in a while went to parties where there was drinking. One night there was a terrible misunderstanding,. . ."

With sympathy in his voice, Walter asked, "You let him divorce you on account of that?"

"No, that—just started things. We kept on living together, because—Bobby was coming."

"Then," asked Walter, "did he leave you flat?"

"No, no." She shook her head. "Jim was fine, Walter. He was crazy about Bobby. And I think Jim lavished on Bobby the love he was losing, or had lost, for me."

"When were you divorced? Just after the kid came?"

"Not for almost a year afterward. We kept up pretenses, and we went out together. One night we went to a party at a studio. I was very unhappy. Jim and I were drifting farther apart. There was wine at the studio, and I drank one glass too many. It was the first time since the time we'd had that terrible quarrel over a year before, that I'd taken *any* kind of a drink, and— well, it hit me hard and sudden."

"You quarreled again, had a real blow-up?"

Mary bit her lip, nodded slowly. "It was awful, Walter. How two people who had loved each other could be so bitter and— But don't blame Jim, Walter. I was nasty, vicious—said things I didn't mean,. . .Jim filed suit for divorce the next day."

Walter Meers clucked in sympathy. "Just like that, eh?"

"Yes," whispered Mary, "just like that. When the case came up in court, I didn't contest it. I just stayed away because if I'd contested it, there'd have been big publicity and it would have hurt Jim's career."

"You let Jim have the kid?"

"What else *could* I do? He loved Bobby as much as I did by

that time, and he wanted him. And I hadn't any money, not even a job. I couldn't have worked as a waitress and brought Bobby up, right." Mary began sobbing very softly.

It made Walter a little uneasy. He wished, now, he'd never asked her about it, because the girl *had* had a rough time of it. But the way she felt, wouldn't it maybe be doing her a favor to blank things out for her?

He stood up. Her hands were over her face, and he took the automatic out of his pocket and held it clubbed by the barrel. One good swing and it would be over with. And below, at the bottom of the bluff, he could hear a train coming up the grade.

He raised the clubbed pistol, . . .

Mary Burke looked up, and tried to scream, but no sound came. She cowered away, raising an arm against the threatened blow. But it didn't descend. Something, someone, had leaped out of the dark cover of the trees behind the bench.

And Walter was staggering back from a blow, trying, as he staggered, to change the pistol around in his hand.

But there wasn't time. Whoever had hit him was running around the end of the bench and—

She must be dreaming this, because it was *Jim!* And Jim's left fist lashed into Walter's face and his right hand grabbed the wrist of Walter's hand that held the pistol, and twisted.

Walter yelled with sudden pain. And then—as Jim reached down for the fallen gun—Walter broke away and ran to the edge of the bluff and started diagonally downward.

She fainted then, when the danger was over. When she came to, Jim was bending over her. He was still here, and it wasn't a dream.

"Feeling better now, Mary?"

"Yes, but—but what happened?"

"He tried to run down the side of the bluff, and fell. There was a train going by, and—Well, never mind the details. He's dead. I think it will be best all the way around if we let him be found there—as an accidental death. Mary—"

"Yes, Jim?"

"I heard what you told Walter, most of it. I was an awful— *Can* you ever forgive me? And come back, to me and Bobby?"

"Why, *of course,* Jim." As simply as that; not even *yes,* but *of course,* as though there had never been a doubt.

And because this, what was happening, was too big even to think about all at once, her mind went back to what had happened, just before Jim had come.

She asked, "But why was Walter going to kill me? And how did *you* get here?"

"He tried to kill me—and Bobby—an hour ago, and thought he had succeeded. You saw him leaving, so he had to kill you. I saw the two of you driving away and tried to follow, but I lost you. Then I remembered about this place and what had happened here once, and somehow I knew he would bring you here. Or maybe it was just a hunch. I had to take the chance."

"But Bobby! You say he tried to *kill Bobby?* Is he—"

"He's fine, and not a hair of his head harmed. Let's go there now. Mrs. Evans, my housekeeper, won't mind—under the circumstances—if I wake him up to talk to you."

Mary's eyes were closed. She said, softly, "To *meet* me, you mean. He won't even remember. But I'll win him back, Jim, and keep him." *And keep you, too,* she added mentally. For she knew that they might quarrel again, some time, but never bitterly as before. They had tasted enough of bitterness, both of them, . . .

It was four o'clock and almost time for the dawn when Officer Sweeny went by in front of the Delaney house again.

And he said, "Tch, tch," to himself, because Jim's car was still there, parked in front. It had been there at twelve, and at two and now at four. This was breaking the law.

Jim Delaney was a nice young fellow, all right, but duty was duty, and Delaney ought to know better anyway.

Besides, curse the luck, it had been the most uneventful night he'd ever put in since he joined the force. And he'd have to have *something* to report, even if it was only a parking violation.

So, a bit regretfully, Officer Sweeny put one of his big brogans on the running board and using his knee for a desk, wrote out a ticket to put on the car.

SATAN'S SEARCH warrant

Big Ben Hayden woke up, not screaming, but wanting to scream. Two ghouls, each taller than a house, had been fighting each other to decide which of them would eat Ben for an hors d'oeuvre, while he had crouched, unable to escape, in a blind alley. A grinning ghost, holding a huge gong in one hand and a thighbone in the other, was refereeing the bout and even now was hammering the gong to indicate the end of the first round. Or had been hammering it until Ben woke up.

His eyes now open, Big Ben sighed with relief at the sight of familiar and friendly things; the luminous dial of his alarm clock on the table next to the bed; beyond it the outlined pane of the window with heavy rain beating hard against the glass.

But *something* was still ringing. Ben reached out to shut off the alarm clock, then remembered that he hadn't turned it on and that anyway its dial said eleven o'clock and that he'd gone to bed only an hour ago. The phone then; he reached across the clock and knocked the phone off the table. Then, with appropriate remarks, he got out of bed, turned on the light, and picked up the phone.

"Ben Hayden talking," he said.

"Cap Rogers, Ben. Listen, can you come down to the station right away? We're in a jam."

Ben's eyes went to the window. In the glass he could see the reflection of himself, a mountainous figure grotesque in awning-stripe pajamas. And, symbolically, the driving rain was beating hard against the reflection. Buckets of cold and unpleasant wet rain.

He said, "Aw, Cap. I just got to sleep and you want me to come down there? On a night like this!"

"Right away, you lummox," said the telephone receiver firmly. "Look, this is a real storm. There've been wrecks all over town and two houses have blown down and the force is going nuts. And the homicide men all went out on a lead on the Yeager business and then this Elkins thing comes in."

Yawning widely, Ben looked at the window pane again and then deliberately averted his eyes from it. "Aw right," he said. "I'll get dressed and be in as soon as I—"

"Hey, wait," cut in Rogers. "Come to think of it, you don't need to come here. I'll give you the dope and you can go right around to the Wescott Apartments from your place. It's nearer."

"That crooks' nest," Ben grunted. "Which of 'em murdered which?"

"Remember Billy Elkins?"

"The slab-happy little dip? Hell, I thought he was in jail."

"Released this afternoon. He's slab-happy now. They just took him in to the morgue. Found him at the bottom of the air-shaft at the Wescott. But it wasn't murder."

"No?"

"Don't look like it, anyway. There were some sheets fastened to a bed in a vacant furnished apartment on the sixth. Looks like he was shinnying down those sheets to burglarize the apartment below. Paul Durban's apartment."

"Funny," said Ben. "Didn't he used to be a sidekick of Durban's? Work for him, too, once in a while?"

"Yeah. Look, you can get the details when you get there. We're putting it on the blotter as accidental death while attempting a felony. But you go 'round there and make a nuisance of yourself, just in case. Talk to Paul Durban, and to Rafe Murro, and to Hoberg. They all live there."

"Billy Elkins had a wife, didn't he? What's about her?"

"You find out," said Rogers. "So long."

Ben put the receiver back on the hook and shivered. Trying not to look out the window, he dressed, putting on his oldest suit. He hesitated a moment before putting on his suit coat, wondering whether to strap on his shoulder holster, weighing the pros and cons of whether to pack a gun. The cons won; the darn thing would get wet and he'd have to take it apart and clean it when he got home.

He didn't phone for a cab because there was a stand around the corner. That was his first mistake, as he discovered as soon as he stepped outside. Before he reached the corner, he was soaking wet, and when he got there, there weren't any cabs at the stand.

Big Ben ducked his head into the wind and started grimly to walk —almost to swim— the six blocks that would take him to the Wescott Apartments. He couldn't get much wetter, anyway. There was a label in his topcoat that said *Waterproof*, but that label was a snare and a delusion on a night like this. The rain drove into his face and neck like water squirted from a hose; it ran down inside and outside his collar, and even seemed to creep up his trouser legs from below. He walked with a squashing sound because the overshoes he had optimistically put on kept the water which had run down inside his shoes from running out again.

But, eventually, he got there. He stood in the lobby a moment to catch his breath, and then rang the janitor's bell. The lock on the inner door clicked and he went in. A sleepy-looking little man in a bathrobe peered out a door at the end of the hallway.

Ben identified himself, and then asked, "Who found the body, and when?"

"Mrs. Craddock heard it hit," said the janitor. "About half-past nine. She lives in 2-A, and she was in the bathroom then and heard a heck of a thud out in the airshaft. So she opens the window and looks down, and there he is right under the window, only a floor down. The airshaft goes down almost to ground level."

"She's the one who phoned the police?"

"I guess so; I didn't even know till they got here. Nobody tells me these things. But if a radiator starts to leak, or a washer on a faucet gets loose, then—"

"Yeah," said Big Ben. "How many apartments open on the airshaft? Have windows on the airshaft, I mean."

"All of 'em. There are four apartments on each floor, see? And they're all laid out alike, so all three rooms of every apartment has windows on the outside. All the bathrooms have windows on the airshaft in the middle, and only the bathrooms. The airshaft's in the middle, and all the bathrooms have windows on—"

"Yeah," said Ben. "You mean the bathrooms have windows on the airshaft. Let's see—there are seven floors and four apartments to a floor, so there'd be twenty-eight apartments, and twenty-eight bathroom windows on the airshaft, huh?"

"That's right. And it was 6-A, over Mrs. Craddock's that he climbed out the window of."

"That'd be a bathroom window," said Ben. "The chief told me the sheets were fastened to a bed. How could he?"

The janitor shook his head. "You got that wrong. I saw it. He took three sheets offa the bed and knotted 'em together and tied 'em to the double faucet on the bathtub, just inside the window."

"Three sheets," said Ben. "That'd take him down two floors at most. He was trying to get in 5-A or 4-A, wouldn't you say?"

"Likely, yeah. But that airshaft's only four feet square. It could have been any of the apartments on the fourth or fifth. He could get down till he had a foot on the windowsill of, say, 5-A, and then step across to one of the other windows. But, yeah, 4-A or 5-A would be the easiest. Paul Durban lives in 5-A."

"Thanks," said Ben. "Guess I'll go there first."

He squashed his way to the automatic elevator and pushed the button to bring down the car. While he waited, he saw the janitor come out with a mop and start work on the big puddle where Ben had stood outside his door. Ben grinned, and called back, "It's raining out, in case you ain't noticed."

The elevator car was down now, but Ben thought of something and paused with the door halfway open. "Hey," he called back. "You remember what time this drizzle started?"

"Started to rain hard about the time the police got here. Let's see—that'd be a quarter of ten. It came up sudden; come to think of it, it hadn't rained at all before then, since this afternoon."

"Oh," said Ben. "Then it wouldn't have been raining at all when he climbed out into the airshaft, would it?"

"I guess not. Nine-thirty—yeah, it started just after that."

Ben got into the elevator and punched the button marked 5. A minute later, he knocked on the door of 5-A.

Paul Durban, sleek in patent-leather hair and a silk dressing gown, looked aghast at the dripping figure on his threshold.

He said, "Migod, Hayden, next time you go swimming, dress for it. Come in, but not very far, and please *don't* sit down. This furniture is mine."

"Oh," said Ben. "They rent these apartments either way?"

"Sure."

"How come you're not down at that club of yours tonight?" Ben asked. He pushed the door shut behind him and leaned against it, looking around. This was the one big room of the apartment. Off it to the left was a small kitchen with a breakfast nook, and to the right was the bedroom, from which would open the door to the bath.

"Monday night," said Durban. "I always take off Monday night, and sometimes Tuesday, too. The place gets along. Glad I did, tonight. With this storm, there won't be enough business to put in your eye."

"What time did you see Billy Elkins last?" Ben asked.

"You mean alive? Haven't seen him since he went to jail a year ago. Since a couple of weeks before that. We had a quarrel at that time."

"Um," said Ben. "Anything serious?"

"Enough," Durban told him. "I found he'd been doing some petty pilfering at the night club. I'd been keeping him going, off and on, for over a year, every time the sledding was tough for him. Then when he—well, you get the idea."

Ben grinned. "Sure, I get the idea. You knew he was a petty dip, but that was all right as long as he didn't dip into your till. No honor among— Skip it. Had he tried to get in touch with you since he got out of stir today?"

"Tonight," said Durban. "A little before nine. I got a call from Tony—he handles things at the club when I'm not there. He said Billy had been there looking for me. When I wasn't there, Tony said, Billy told him he'd come around here to see me. Tony told him I wouldn't be home, but Billy was coming anyway. He didn't believe Tony."

"Um," said Ben. "But he decided to come in the bathroom window instead of the front door. That was the way you figure it?"

"Seems like it. Anyway, about fifteen minutes after Tony called to warn me Billy was coming, my doorbell rang. It's a fifteen minute walk from here to the club, so I knew who it was, and I didn't answer it."

"So he figured you weren't home, and it'd be a good time to pull a spot of burglary, huh? But instead of that, you were giving him the runaround."

"Call it that if you want," said Durban. "I was through with him. I told him a year ago I was washed up with him and kicked him out. He had a nerve to try to see me at all."

Ben nodded. "Guess you're right, at that. Well, it seems to make sense. Fifteen minutes or so after he thinks he finds you ain't home, he plops down the airshaft. How could he have known the flat above here was empty, though?"

"He could tell that from the mailbox, in the lobby. All but the vacant ones got names on them."

"Yeah," said Ben. "Who else lives here in the building had any contact with Elkins, that you know of?"

"Murro," said Durban. "Rafael Murro, down on the third floor. Murro was Billy's lawyer when they put him away last year. Did a good job of getting him off with that sentence."

"You figure maybe he'd have rung Murro's bell when nobody answered yours?"

Durban shrugged.

"Well, I'll ask Murro anyway," said Ben. "Anybody else?"

"Frank Hoberg. Used to do a little business with Billy, or so I've heard. Don't quote me on it."

Big Ben didn't ask what kind of business. Hoberg was a fence; he knew that.

Instead he asked, "What about Mitzie, Billy's wife? Know what she's doing lately or where she stays?"

"I don't," said Durban. "She came to see me just after Billy got sent up. She wanted a job as a cigarette girl at the club, and I gave it to her. She was a good kid and I didn't figure I should take it out on her just because Billy was a rat. She held the job for—let's see—maybe eight months, and then quit. I haven't seen her since."

"Say why she was quitting?"

"I wasn't there the night it happened, but she had a blow-up with Tony about something or other. She said she had a better job offered her anyway and walked out."

"Job or proposition? Or could you guess?"

"I don't know. Far as I know—up to four months ago anyway—she was still carrying a torch for Billy."

"Who'd know where she is now?" Ben asked.

"Murro might. As Billy's lawyer, he ought to know."

"Thanks," said Ben. "I'll go see him. By the way, is blackmail still a sideline with Murro, or has it crowded his law practice into the background by now?"

"I wouldn't know," said Durban. "He never had anything on me. Shall I send the bill for a new rug to the department, or to you personally?"

"Send it to Cap Rogers," said Ben. "He sent me out in this tonight. And split with me if he pays; it hurts me more than it does your rug. Well, so long."

Going back down to the lobby, Ben studied the rows of mailboxes, confirming what Durban had told him—6-A, above Durban, was vacant—7-A, above that, was labeled Frank Hoberg. But that couldn't mean anything in particular. You couldn't get into 7-A from the empty apartment below it with knotted sheets; not unless you could do the Hindu rope trick.

He went back in—he'd left the door ajar with a pencil stuck in to keep it from closing—and took the elevator up to the sixth.

Everything in 6-A seemed to be on the up and up. Three sheets had been yanked off the bed. Knotted together, they were tied to the heavy faucet fixture of the bathtub, which was right under the airshaft window. Someone had pulled them back inside, but hadn't untied them. They were still wet.

He opened the window and leaned out to look down. Couldn't see anything down there, but then there'd be nothing to see anyway. The body was taken away and the rain that was now running down the back of his neck had washed away any stains.

He closed the window and went down to 3-B. Rafael Murro let him in without any evidence of pleasure at seeing him.

"About Billy Elkins," said Big Ben. "When'd you see him last?"

"Few weeks ago," Murro told him. "At the jail. I kept in touch with him, of course."

"When'd you see his wife last?"

"Last week, I believe."

"Where's she living and what's she doing?"

Murro said, "She's staying at the Indiana Hotel—or was then. I don't know what she's doing. That's none of my business."

"Um," said Ben. "Not if it's honest, it ain't. You didn't see Elkins today, since he got out? Nor hear from him?"

"No."

"Know any reason why Bill Elkins would have seen, or tried to see, Frankie Hoberg?"

"No."

"Um," said Ben again. He took off his hat and looked at it, and then put it on again. There was something about this case he didn't like. It was too simple, too pat. Everything fitted, except that in a building lousy with potential murderers, a guy like Elkins had to get himself accidentally killed.

He tried a fresh tack. He said, "Billy Elkins was a small-time punk, and your services come high. Or so I'm told. You worked hard on Billy's case. You got him off in a year, and otherwise it'd have been ten. Where'd he ever get the kind of sugar you'd ask for doing that?"

Murro shrugged. "My fee wasn't high. He paid it, and it's not my business where he got the money."

"It ought to've been our business," said Ben. "We should have looked into it at the time. But wait a minute. Suppose he didn't pay you—in money."

"I don't know what you mean."

"Sure, you do. Blackmail. Billy Elkins didn't have any money, but why couldn't he have given you something that would have let you put the screws on somebody that had dough?"

The lawyer smiled. "An interesting theory," he said.

"Um," said Big Ben. "The more you think of it, the more interesting it gets. It wouldn't have been Durban; Durban's legitimate. He makes enough out of his night club that I don't think he has a racket. But Elkins did business with Hoberg. He could have put the finger on Hoberg, couldn't he?"

"I wouldn't know."

"I wouldn't either," said Ben, "but I aim to find out. I'm going to use your phone, if you don't mind—or even if you do. I think Elkins' death outside your window is enough of an excuse that I can get somebody sent down here with a search warrant." He was squashing his way across the room toward the telephone while he talked. "And maybe if I stick around until the warrant gets here—"

"Take him, Pete." It was Murro's voice, and it was hard as ice. Just before Big Ben Hayden got to the phone.

"Up, copper," said another voice, and Ben raised his hands slowly as he turned.

A dark, stocky man Ben had never seen before stood in the doorway that led to the bedroom. He held a revolver with a silencer on its barrel, aimed at Ben.

"Hold it," said Murro. He took down a picture from the wall and spun the dial of a safe that had been behind it. He thrust into his pocket a small bundle of papers that he took from the safe, and then closed it again.

He said, "We'll have to take the copper for a ride, Pete. I should have had sense enough to get these things out of here before, after we found out Elkins broke his damn neck. We'll have to stash them somewhere else, too."

"Okay," said the man he'd called Pete. "Look, step behind him and frisk him, will you, Rafe?"

Murro came around behind Ben, felt his hip pockets and side pockets first, and then stepped in close to reach around front. He had to stand close to do that; it took a man with long arms to encircle Big Ben Hayden's girth. Murro's hands felt his vest pockets, and that meant Murro was standing very close to him and he could feel Murro's breath on the back of his neck.

Ben's hands were shoulder high, and he'd bent his elbows so they were in close to his neck — and to Murro's head.

This, Ben had a hunch, was going to be the best chance he'd be likely to get to make a break. And he took it.

He moved with a suddeness that few would have believed possible in a man of his dimensions. His upraised hands darted back over his shoulders and clamped on the sides of the lawyer's head, and the instant those hands made contact with their objective, Ben threw his weight forward from the waist, hurling Murro over Ben's head, into the gunman and the gun.

The silenced pistol was coughing dryly. Twice it coughed and then there was a thud that shook the walls, another thud, and silence.

Ben looked first at the man whose hand still held the pistol, and then at the lawyer. He put a pudgy hand on the chest of each of them, over where the heartbeat should have been. Then he went across the room to the telephone, and called Captain Rogers.

He said, "This is Ben. I'm in Rafe Murro's apartment. Better send the wagon."

"What happened?"

"All of a sudden, murder," said Ben. "Guy named Pete shot Rafe Murro in the head with a pistol. Bullet went straight in from the top and straight down. You'll probably find it somewhere down around his ankles."

"The hell! And the killer—have you got—"

"Then Rafe went ahead and killed this here Pete," said Ben. "He slammed into him going ninety miles an hour and knocked Pete backwards and Pete's head took a big chunk of wood out of the door jamb. It didn't do Pete's head any good either. So you can book 'em for killing each other."

"You kidding me, Ben? How could—"

"You'll see when you get here, Cap. Or whenever whoever you send gets here. And listen, in Rafe Murro's pocket, there's going to be plenty evidence to tie him up to the blackmail we figured he was pulling. I threw a scare in him by talking about a search warrant, and he got tough."

"Did he have anything to do with Elkins' death, Ben?"

"I dunno, Cap. I'm still working on that. I'm going to keep on working on it, but I'll be around the building somewhere when the wagon gets here. Look, what was the result of the examination on Billy Elkins?"

"Killed instantly. That was a narrow shaft, and he hit his head on a couple window sills on the way down. We found blood on them. If you want a list of all the bones fractured—"

"I don't," said Ben. "I'll take your word for it. What all was in his pockets? Did he have any money or was he broke?"

"Just some small change. But he sure had a lot of other stuff in his pockets. Want to hear the list?"

"Sure," said Ben. "Read it, will you?"

Ben listened closely, and whistled. Then he put the receiver back on the hook and looked up the phone number of the Indiana Hotel.

A sleepy voice answered.

"Mitzie Elkins, please," said Ben.

"She checked out today."

Ben said, "That's funny. I had an appointment with her. Did she say where she was going, or give any forwarding address?"

"No. She left rather hurriedly this morning and said she'd give us an address later. If she gets in touch with us, who shall I tell her called?"

"Her husband," said Ben. "This is Billy Elkins. Sure she didn't leave any message for me?"

"No, she didn't."

"Funny," said Ben, and he put the receiver back on the hook. It *was* funny. Mitzie Elkins must have learned this morning that her husband was getting out of jail in the afternoon. And if she was still in love with him, she'd taken a funny way of showing it.

There was a decanter of whiskey on the table. Murro hadn't offered Ben a drink, but he figured Murro wouldn't mind now. So he had one. It made him feel warm inside and that made him realize how cold and wet the outside of him still was.

Dammit, why couldn't he make up his mind that Billy Elkins had simply fallen down that airshaft? It made sense.

But the farther he got into this case, the farther there was to go. Now he'd have to find out why Mitzie had run out this morning. Maybe have to go sloshing out in the rain again, hunting her.

And he'd have to see Frankie Hoberg and ask him—

Hey! How about those papers that were in Murro's pocket? Maybe there was a lead there to the Elkins business.

Ben went over and got the papers, glanced through them. There were leads, in those papers, to lots of things that Cap Rogers would find interesting. Things that—

Then, on the second last one, he caught a glimpse of the signature, "Wm. Elkins." Ben read it carefully, and said, "I'll be damned. Right on the head!"

And he wondered vaguely if he'd been psychic. He'd taken a random shot in the dark by asking Murro if Billy Elkins had paid him off in material for blackmail against Hoberg. It had been a bull's-eye.

The paper he had in his hand was a confession signed by Elkins, which incriminated Hoberg as the fence who handled everything Billy had stolen. Signing that confession, then, had been the price Billy had paid for Murro's services in getting a ten-year sentence divided by ten. Did Mitzie know he'd signed? She must have.

And Hoberg would know, of course. That knowledge would have cost him plenty of sugar. Then Hoberg *did* have a motive for killing Elkins.

The paper still in his hand, Ben strolled over to the window and stared out into the rain. Maybe Hoberg had—

The Black Maria was pulling up, out in front. Two men with yellow slickers over blue uniforms got out and ran toward the door, and a few seconds later, Murro's doorbell buzzed. Ben went over and pushed the button that would unlatch the door.

Then, on a sudden impulse, he slipped the paper incriminating Hoberg into his own pocket and the others back into Murro's. Dammit, he might as well follow through with that paper now, and get it over with. Then he could swim back home, take a hot bath, and get back to bed.

He heard the elevator start up, had another quick snort of Murro's whiskey, and then let the patrolmen in the door. He said, "Hi, boys. Nothing for you to do but take these two mugs to the morgue. It's under control. But there are some important papers in the guy's pocket. See that they don't get lost, and that Rogers gets them."

"Okay, Ben. You're coming in with us, aren't you?"

Ben shook his head. "This was a sideline. Me, I'm still worrying about a guy falling down an airshaft. Tell Rogers I'll phone him again later."

"But he said you was to come in with us and explain about these guys and—"

"Tell him also, nuts," said Ben. "I want to get this over with so I can go home."

He went down to the elevator, got in, and punched the button for the top floor, the seventh.

He knocked on the door of 7-A. He didn't know Hoberg, but he'd heard him described, and he recognized the ratty little man who opened the door as fitting the description.

"Police," he said. "Want to talk to you, Hoberg."

Hoberg hesitated only a second, then opened the door wide enough for Ben to step through. Ben did, and wished he hadn't. There were two other men in the room, and they both looked tough. Hoberg he could have broken with one hand, but the other two men looked like ex-pugs. Ben wished now that he'd borrowed a gun from one of the men who'd come with the wagon. But he hadn't thought of it, then.

"This says it's a copper, boys," said Hoberg to the two men. "It wants to talk to me."

"Yeah," said Ben. "About Billy Elkins. He fell down your airshaft tonight. Suppose you've heard about it."

"Sure," said Hoberg. He looked relieved, and became suddenly less belligerent. "Sure, I heard about it. When I got home. I—we were out then."

"When was this?"

"Happened at nine-thirty, didn't it? That's what I heard. Me and my pals here didn't get home till after ten. And if you think it ain't an alibi, think again. We were in night court. Benny and Dutch were in a little trouble, and I bailed them out."

"Sounds good," said Ben. "What time'd you leave there?"

"Not till almost ten. Ask Judge Steinke, or the court clerk." Hoberg grinned.

"Steinke's good enough for me," said Ben. "I'll check with him later. Seen Billy Elkins since he got out?"

"No."

"Or Mitzie?"

"Hell, no. That wren's poison. Billy was nuts about her; he'd have stuck a shiv in anyone that looked at her."

"I have a hunch," said Ben, "that somebody's been looking at her plenty. You wouldn't know who?"

"I wouldn't," said Hoberg. "I haven't seen her around since she quit working at Durban's place three months or so ago."

"Okay, Hoberg," said Ben. "Guess you're clean on the Elkins business. But you'll have to come with me to the station just the same. We've got another charge against you."

"The hell you have. You coppers ain't got a thing—" Hoberg stared incredulously at Ben. "Or did that louse Morro—"

"Murro's dead," said Ben. He could have bit his tongue the moment he said it. Definitely, it was the wrong thing. If he'd kept his yap shut, Hoberg would have come along without a struggle. He'd have figured it was a rap he could beat, nothing worth trying to shoot his way out of. But now there was a mean-looking little thirty-two in Hoberg's hand, and Hoberg stepped forward and held it against Ben's chest.

"Hey," said one of the ex-pugs uneasily. "Go easy, Frankie. That's a copper and we don't want to be tangled in—"

"Shut up," said Hoberg. "If Murro's dead, then maybe this guy's got—" His free left hand had first tapped Ben's pockets for a revolver, and then it slid into Ben's inside coat pocket and came out with the folded paper that was Billy Elkins' confession. Without letting the gun waver, he partly unfolded it and glanced at the signature. He sucked in his breath and let it out audibly, as he crumpled the paper into his own pocket.

He said, "Benny, Dutch. We got to take this copper out and—"

The mugs were standing now, behind Hoberg. One of them said, "Nuts, Frankie. This is your business, not ours. Why should we stick our heads into a noose just because—"

"You got to," yelled Hoberg. "You got to help me, because I got plenty on both of you. How about that St. Louis business where the two guards got—"

Something black and heavy rose in the air behind Hoberg's head, and descended. Hoberg dropped, and Ben—who had seen it coming—tried to grab at the gun that had been in Hoberg's hand. But missed.

"Hold it," said one of the two men, and the black automatic whose butt had hit Hoberg was now trained on Ben Hayden. The other man bent down over the huddled figure of Hoberg.

He said, "You stopped his clock."

"Hell," said the one with the gun. "We might as well've played along in the first place. Now *we* got to rub out the copper. Hell."

Ben said reasonably, "You don't have to kill me if you don't want to. You can tie me up. You'll have to lam anyway; they'll find out you were here with Hoberg. He was with you in court half an hour ago. And he wasn't any loss to society, but if you kill a cop—"

"Nuts," said the man with the gun. "Hoberg was a rat, but they use as many volts on you for killing a rat as—"

The other of the two mugs stood up. He had Hoberg's gun in his left hand, and he'd been frisking Hoberg's pockets with the other. He said, "Twenty lousy bucks. We're broke, and that's all the louse has on him. We'll have to lam on twenty lousy bucks."

Funny, Ben thought, how crooks ran true to type. Now, in the middle of danger and murder, their first thought was of what they could walk off with. The eyes of the man who'd just frisked Hoberg were even now darting around the room, looking for something valuable enough to steal. Just as Billy Elkins, fresh out of jail, had stolen. . . .

Ben grunted. He said, "I got twelve bucks. Might as well tell you. You'll find it anyway, when you tie me up."

The one who'd killed Hoberg said, "Hold that gun on him, Dutch. I'll take his dough." He moved sidewise around Ben, and Ben caught the glint in his eye and knew that they weren't going to tie him up. That this was a stall.

They didn't want to shoot off a gun and raise a ruckus, and this guy—if the other was Dutch, this must be Benny, his namesake—was making an excuse to get behind him and kill him the same way he'd killed Hoberg.

And there wouldn't be room to try the trick he'd worked on Murro. Benny wouldn't stand that close to hit him, and Dutch was off to one side anyway, with Hoberg's thirty-two aimed at Ben Hayden's belt buckle.

Ben said, "Wait a minute, Benny. Listen, I got an idea."

"Yeah? What?"

The odd thing was that he *did* have an idea. An idea that had come to him while he watched Dutch's eyes wander around the room looking for something to swipe. A long-shot idea, or was it? It started out that Billy Elkins was a dip, maybe even a kleptomaniac type of dip. And it went on that Billy'd stick a shiv— according to Hoberg—into anyone who looked cross-eyed at Mitzie Elkins.

"Five hundred dollars or five thousand dollars—whatever the guy's got on him or can raise quick. How'd you like to have that much money for your getaway? Within a matter of minutes from now?"

"From who?"

Ben said, "From the man who dropped Billy Elkins down the airshaft."

"Nuts," said the one called Benny. "The copper's just trying to talk his way out of a jam. He's stalling. Go ahead and—"

Dutch said, "Shut up. The guy's talking money. Just maybe he's got something. All right, copper, speak your piece. How would we get this five grand?"

Ben said, "The man who killed Elkins pays you. The three of us go down there. I'm not heeled, and you both are, so you needn't worry about a break. I convince Durban—yeah, Paul Durban killed Elkins—that I can prove a murder rap on him. Then you talk business with him."

"You think he'd pay us—"

"Sure. Take him for whatever dough he's got, for which you agree to save his neck by taking me for a ride. That gives you money to pull your freight on. Then you let me out on a deserted road somewhere and keep traveling. You've got to stage a getaway, don't you? And with real money, you can do that."

"It's risky, but— Listen, copper, if you double-cross us, there ain't a chance it'll do you any good. If anything goes wrong, we shoot *you* first. We got nothing to lose; we already—" He nodded toward what was left of Frank Hoberg.

"Sure," said Big Ben. "Let's get going."

"We better use the stairs," Dutch said. "Okay, copper, we don't have to trust you. This heater'll be in your back all the way. Go ahead."

The stairway was only a few steps from the door of 7-A. They saw no one in the hallway, nor in the hallway of the fifth floor.

Ben Hayden knocked on Durban's door. When it opened, the three of them pushed their way past Durban into the apartment. Dutch closed the door and leaned against it.

Ben said, "Paul, here are a couple of boys who want to talk business with you—after I get through."

Durban looked puzzled, and annoyed. He said, "After you get through what?"

"Talking," said Ben. "I'm starting now. I know why you killed Elkins and how to prove it. You were playing around with Mitzie. You gave her the cigarette girl job at your club, until you talked her into giving it up and letting you install her at a hotel. Then when Billy got out of jail today, you knew he'd find out sooner or later, even though Mitzie had gone into hiding this morning, before he got out. And you knew Billy would kill you when he found out."

"I told you, Hayden, I hadn't seen Mitzie for—"

"Nuts. All we have to do is take you around to the Indiana Hotel for identification by employees or other guests there. If I'm right, it'll be easy to prove it.

"But here's what happened tonight. Billy hadn't found out yet. He was still looking for Mitzie, and he wanted to see you to make a touch. He tried the club, and then came here. You *did* answer the bell, and let him come up. Then, the way I figure it, he must have been in here alone for a short while. Dunno how that happened, but I'll make one guess.

"You wanted something to kill him with that wouldn't make a noise or a mark. So you went in the bathroom awhile, and you put a cake of soap in the toe of a sock. That makes a good blackjack. Then you came back and—

"Well, you could have killed him here, but you'd have had to carry him to the flat above. My guess is you got him up there on some pretext and slugged him there. Then you rigged the sheets out of the window and dropped him down the airshaft."

Paul Durban didn't smile; there wasn't any expression on his face at all. He said, "That's guesswork, Hayden. Now get the hell out of—"

"Shut up," said Dutch.

"You forgot something, Paul. When you left Elkins in here, you forgot he was a petty dip, maybe a klepto to boot. You say he was never in here. Well, there's proof that he was. Pocketfuls of it. Elkins' pockets were full of stuff he swiped when you left him alone.

"He stepped into the kitchenette—there's silverware to prove it. And your bureau's just inside the bedroom door and he had time to reach through and loot it—the top of it anyway. Studs and cufflinks and stuff. And a gold watch. There was an initial G on it, and that didn't hit me right away.

"But didn't you originally have a name like—wasn't it Golemononavian or something like that? And didn't you change it for business reasons when you opened a club of your own? If we can prove that watch was yours, let alone the rest of the stuff he'd swiped—well, you see where it puts you, since you're on record he didn't come here."

Dutch had stepped forward alongside Ben Hayden while he was talking. His gun was still aimed at Ben; the other man's gun still covered Durban.

Ben said, "Okay, boys. It's your turn. I think he'll talk business."

Dutch's greedy eyes, as well as those of the other gunman, swung to Durban's face.

Ben's big hand lashed out and down at the gun in Dutch's hand, not trying to grab it, but slapping the gun and the hand that held it—with pile-driver force. The gun hit the hardwood floor.

The other gunman was swinging Hoberg's thirty-two around from Durban to Ben, and pulling the trigger. It went off a fraction of a second too soon, just before the muzzle had completed its arc. And he didn't have time to trigger it again, for Big Ben's fist exploded in his face.

Ben changed the blow to a grab, and when he wheeled back around, his hands were full of unconscious gunman. Dutch, his face gray with pain and his right arm hanging as though the wrist were broken, was stooping to pick up the fallen gun with his left hand.

Ben threw his gunman namesake, Benny, at Dutch. And then whirled to Durban.

Ben said, "It was a free fight, Paul. We'd have liked to have had you in on it."

Durban tried to smile, but it was a sickly effort. He said, "I'd rather take my chances with a jury, Hayden. You play too damn rough."

Ben grunted. He picked the two pistols off the floor and then walked over to the telephone. . . .

Captain Rogers was scowling. He said, "Dammit, Ben, we send you to check a simple burglary. You find it's murder, and get the killer, and that's all right. But why, on a night like this, d'you got to start so much trouble we get three *more* stiffs? Murro, and Pete, and Hoberg. And *three* guys in on murder raps instead of one.

"On top of it, one with a broken arm and one with a broken jaw, so we got to handle them careful. And enough material in those papers on Murro to keep us busy a week.

"Anyhow, I commandeered the last free taxicab in town; it's out front. Take it home and get those wet clothes off and go back to sleep. Tomorrow you'll be a hero, but tonight you're in my hair."

DEATH INSURANCE *payment*

Mr. Henry Smith strode briskly along the sidewalk as far as the property line of the big house at 814 Vista Lane. There he frowned slightly and paused, for the snow had not yet been shoveled off the walk, although it was almost ten o'clock in the morning.

And as number 814 was the third-last house on a dead-end street, only a few people had walked by to trample a very narrow path through the seven inches of snow.

With something of the air of a tightrope walker, Mr. Smith negociated the narrow path until he reached the point where a walk led back from the sidewalk to the porch. Here Mr. Smith paused again and said, "Tch, tch." For that walk was also unshoveled and not a single footprint marred its virgin whiteness.

Mr. Smith sighed and turned up the cuffs of his neat pinstriped trousers before he walked back toward the porch. It had turned colder since the snow had fallen last night. The slight crust that had formed atop the snow broke crunchingly with each step he took.

179

On the porch, he brushed the snow very carefully from his ankles and shoe tops, turned down his trouser cuffs, wiped his overshoes on the mat and then removed them; all before he pressed the bell button.

Nothing happened for a while and he pressed it again. And later, a third time. Then there was the sound of a window opening upstairs and a voice—a male voice—called out, "Whoozit?"

Mr. Smith walked to the end of the porch and looked up. A young man with tousled hair was leaning out of the window. He wore a bathrobe and had apparently just got out of bed.

"My name is Henry Smith," said Mr. Henry Smith. "I have an appointment with Mr. Gaby, at ten o'clock."

"Uh," said the young man at the window. "Maybe he overslept. I did, if it's that late. But I wonder why Larkin didn't—Oh, hell. Waitaminit. I'll be down and let you in."

He closed the window and a few minutes later opened the front door. He said, "Come on in. I'll go see if the old boy's still asleep or what? You're sure there isn't any mistake about the appointment—the time of it, I mean?"

"I talked to Mr. Gaby over the phone yesterday," said Mr. Smith. "He was very definite about the time, so it's odd—uh—who is this Larkin you mentioned?"

"Servant. The only one. He'd have answered the bell if he's here, so I guess he went out marketing or something. Say, you're the insurance fellow, aren't you?"

Mr. Smith nodded. His gold-rimmed pince-nez glasses were steaming up, so he took them off and polished them on a white silk handkerchief from his breast pocket.

"I am connected with the Phalanx Life Insurance Company. Yes. Mr. Gaby said he wished to take out a policy on someone—not on himself, I believe."

The young man nodded. "On his daughter—my wife. My name's Standish—Roy Standish. Mr. Gaby's son-in-law. We're just here visiting. Beth's father said something about taking a policy on her while she was— Well, take off your coat and sit down. I'll go see if Mr. Gaby's still asleep."

He started upstairs. Mr. Smith took off his overcoat and hung it neatly on a hook of the hatrack. Then, rubbing his hands together to warm them, he looked about him curiously.

Two doors off the large hallway in which he stood were closed, a third leading to a passageway toward the back of the house was open. Mr. Smith glanced down the passage past two more doors and a butler's pantry and found himself looking into the open doorway of a kitchen.

From that direction came the sound of a knock. Mr. Smith hesitated a moment, then walked through into the kitchen. The knocking came from the back door.

Mr. Smith crossed a very disordered kitchen, with dishes piled in the sink and on the table, and glasses and bottles very much in evidence, and opened the back door. A boy of about twelve stood there, a snow shovel in his hand. He tipped his cap politely.

He said, "Shovel your walk, mister?"

Mr. Smith peered out over the boy's head at the single line of footprints that led back to the alley. They were small footprints.

Mr. Smith sighed. He said, "I'm afraid it isn't my sidewalk. No. Maybe if you come back later. . ."

Mr. Smith closed the door and through the glass pane watched him start back toward the alley.

Then Mr. Smith turned around and looked again, more closely, at the messy kitchen, and rubbed his hands together again to warm them. It was quite cool. Certainly not over sixty degrees.

If it was Larkin's duty to fire the furnace, he had been re-miss in that as well as in straightening up the kitchen. Dishes piled high, closet door ajar—

Mr. Smith crossed over to that closet and opened the door wider.

And if the man on the floor of the closet was Larkin, it was quite obvious why he had not straightened the kitchen or fired the furnace. He was dead, quite dead.

Gingerly, Mr. Henry Smith touched the cold flesh of the man's face to be sure, then he walked rapidly back through the passageway to the front hall. Roy Standish was just coming down the stairs.

He said, "Funny, but the old boy isn't in his room—and his bed hasn't been slept in. I woke up Beth and Tommy, but they don't know anything about—"

"Tommy? Who is Tommy?"

"Tommy Lee, Beth's cousin, Mr. Gaby's nephew. Here visit-ing, too. Regular family reunion. But they don't know—"

"I am very much afraid," said Mr. Henry Smith, "that some-thing unpleasant has happened. There is a dead man in the kitchen closet. Small, about my build, elderly, bald. Would that be—?"

"Larkin. *Dead?* Are you sure? We'd better phone for a doc—"

"He is quite dead," said Mr. Smith. "Dead for some hours, I would say, for cadaveric rigidity is moderately advanced. I fear we must telephone the police."

"The police? You mean—"

"There is a faint odor of—ah—bitter almonds," said Mr. Smith. "That and the fact that the body is partially tied up with rope and a gag has been used— When did you see your father-in-law last?"

"About two o'clock, when we went to bed. Why? You don't think—?"

"I do not yet know just what I think," said Mr. Smith. "But if Mr. Gaby was in this house at two o'clock this morning, he is still in it."

"How—how do you know that?"

"It stopped snowing before midnight," said Mr. Smith. "And there are no footprints in the snow that could be his. In front, only mine. And at the back, only those of a boy who came just now to ask if he might shovel the walks."

"Good gosh, then—"

Roy Standish looked at the closed door immediately across the hall, went to it, and opened it. Again he said, "Good gosh!"

Mr. Smith was right behind him, but unable to see over the taller man's shoulder until Standish went on into the room. And then his attention was distracted by a woman's voice from the top of the stairs. "Roy, is anything wrong?"

Mr. Smith turned. An attractive dark-haired woman of about thirty, wearing a navy blue housecoat, was coming down the steps.

"Mrs. Standish?" he said. "Yes, something is wrong. I would suggest that you remain upstairs until—"

"Beth," said Standish, coming out of the room across the hall, "your father's dead. And Larkin, too. We've got to phone—"

Mr. Smith cleared his throat. It had not escaped his sharp small eyes that although there was surprise and shock registered upon the faces of Mr. Gaby's daughter and his son-in-law, there was little, if any grief for the departed. Mr. Gaby could not have been very popular with his relatives.

He said, "I will phone the police for you, Mr. Standish. I am quite well acquainted with Captain Krasno of the homicide squad. I sold him a large policy recently. Meanwhile, you people will have just time to dress, if you wish, before the police get here."

The telephone was already in his hand, and he said, "Police headquarters, please," into the mouthpiece.

Captain Krasno asked, "This body's just like you found it?"

"Except that I didn't find it, yes," said Mr. Smith. "It was I who found the other body but not this one. I was in the hall outside this door. Mr. Standish went in first. Then his wife, Mr. Gaby's daughter, started to come down the stairs and I turned to speak to her and—"

"And this Standish guy come in here alone?"

"Well," said Mr. Smith judiciously, "he did step just inside the door, but he left it open. I don't believe he had time to change anything in the—uh—setup, if that's what you mean, Captain."

Mr. Smith polished his gold-rimmed glasses very carefully and then looked again at the body of Mr. Gaby. It was seated in a Morris chair beside a library table on which a book lay open. Perhaps "seated" is not quite the correct word, for it was doubled far forward in the chair, the head almost between the knees.

The lamp beside the chair was still lighted, Mr. Smith saw, and then his eyes went to the table again and the decanter of whiskey upon it. There was no glass on the table, but the glass was plainly in evidence on the floor beside the chair.

"I presume," said Mr. Smith, "that the whiskey is poisoned with prussic acid."

"You presume damn well right," Krasno said. "Enough poison to kill a brigade. Whoever did it sure didn't appreciate how little of that stuff he needed."

"Or perhaps," said Mr. Smith, "he was merely generous. Have you found the bottle the prussic acid was in?"

Krasno nodded glumly. "On the kitchen sink, empty, but it had prussic acid in it, all right. Right next to the empty whiskey bottle."

"Ah," said Mr. Smith.

"What you mean, ah?"

"I mean that whoever adminstered the poisoned whiskey to Mr. Gaby, mixed it in the kitchen and brought it in to him here. Mr. Gaby was reading and put down his book to take a drink."

Krasno snorted. "And took the drink and decided not to pick up the book again."

Mr. Smith ignored the sarcasm. "Exactly," he said. "And did you notice what the book is? It deals with insurance. Life insurance. Undoubtedly considering just what type of policy he was going to purchase for his daughter."

"Murder," said Krasno. "We're talking about murder, not insurance. Hey, though; did Gaby carry any?"

Mr. Smith shook his head sadly. "Chronic heart trouble. He couldn't pass an examination. It is unfortunate but necessary that insurance companies protect themselves by refusing to issue policies to—"

"Heart trouble," said Krasno. "Huh. Well, he sure didn't die of that. How rich was he?"

"Just well-to-do. I believe his investments brought him about twenty-thousand a year, clear of taxes. A very sound business head, too. Which is amply proven by the fact that he intended to take a policy on his daughter. Probably a single-pay life. In these days of changing fortunes, a policy of that kind is—"

"Listen," said Krasno, "don't you ever think of anything but life insurance?"

"Of course," said Mr. Smith. "We sell fire insurance, too. We have a policy on this house, in effect for eight years. And that reminds me, Captain, I don't believe I've ever discussed fire insurance with you. Is your house— Oh, that's right, you live in a flat."

"I live in a flat," said Krasno. "And right now I'm investigating a murder. Two murders. And yet I got to listen to you talk about insur—"

"Cap, the photographers are here," called out a voice from the hallway. "Which you want 'em to take first?"

"This one in here," said Krasno. "C'mon, let's get out and give them room. You can go on home, Mr. Smith."

"Thank you," said Mr. Smith gravely and followed the captain into the kitchen.

The captain paused at the closet, but Mr. Smith went on over to the sink.

"Ah, yes," he said. "That would be the bottle from which the prussic acid came. And there's the whiskey bottle. And it looks as though he mixed them by pouring both into the decanter and then, possibly, shaking it. Spilled some, too. Did you notice that big white spot on the green paint of the sink? He was careless."

"He or she."

"She?"

"Sure," said Krasno. "There's only three people who could've done it, no? This Standish and Lee and Standish's wife. Had to be one of those three on account of what you tell me about the snow. Nobody else was here."

"No? Mr. Gaby and Larkin were here."

"Yeah, sure. They murdered each other. But seriously, any one of those three had motive, because they're all heirs. And we found out one thing; the old guy had phoned his lawyer and had an appointment for this afternoon. He was going to make some change in his will. If we knew what change—"

"His lawyer?" said Mr. Smith. "That would be Mr. Bergen of Henderson and Bergen, wouldn't it?"

"It would," said Krasno. "And I suppose you know him well, because you sold him an insurance policy on his life and— Why don't you beat it, dammit?"

"No," said Mr. Smith gravely. "The policy I sold Mr. Bergen was on his house." He sighed. "He, too, failed to pass an examination. Did he tell you all the provisions of the will?"

"Weren't many. Gaby left five thousand each to three charities, five thousand to Larkin, and the rest to be divided equally between his daughter and his nephew."

Mr. Smith pursed his lips. "Strange; one would think he would leave the lion's share to his own offspring. But possibly—"

"Yeah, they didn't get along so hot. He liked this nephew, Tommy Lee, better. And from what I judge, there wasn't too much love lost there, either. He was a tight-fisted old skin-flint, according to everybody I've talked to."

Mr. Smith sighed again. "I fear I must agree. In my dealings with him about the insurance on this property— Yes, I fear the criticisms of him are well taken and that his relatives will not mourn him unduly."

Krasno grunted. He said, "What gets me is why they started to tie this guy Larkin up and never finished. Hey" —Lieutenant Brady had just come in the door— "look at this, Pete. His ankles tied up and a piece of rope cut to fit his wrists but never put on. And gagged, too. Why didn't whoever tied him up, finish the job?"

Brady took off his hat and scratched his head. "I been wondering that, Cap. But what I wonder most is why they ever started to tie him up at all."

"Keep him out of the way while they killed Gaby."

"Yeah, but he was already dead. Must've been dead, because prussic's instantaneous."

"Uh—that's right. And they could kill him or tie him up, but why do both? It don't make sense."

Brady said, "How about this? They started to tie him up and then decide to poison him instead and force the poison on him."

Mr. Henry Smith smiled. "A question, Lieutenant. Did they poison him, then, before or after they put the gag on him?"

"Why, before, of— Uh, yeah. That's right, Cap. They could have tied his ankles before he was poisoned, but they'd have to put that damn gag on afterwards. And why did they do that— and not finish tying up his hands? It don't make any sense at all."

"Yeah," Krasno growled. "You check the bottles and glasses and stuff for fingerprints?"

"None on the whiskey bottle or the prussic bottle. Just Gaby's on the decanter and on the glass he drank out of. All other prints were wiped clean, off everything."

"Nuts. Well, we're still sure it's one of three people. Got to be. And all of 'em got motives."

Brady sighed deeply. "We've been questioning them and don't get anywhere, except that the Standishes alibi one another pretty thoroughly. If one of them done it, they were in it together. Then there's this Tommy Lee, he was by himself. But his story fits with theirs as far as it goes."

"What was their story, Lieutenant?" Mr. Smith asked.

"That they all three of them went upstairs to turn in a little after one o'clock. They'd been talking and all doing a little drinking, mostly wine, but not enough to be tight or anything. Old Man Gaby stayed downstairs; said he was going to read a while before he turned in. And the other three of them say they went to bed and that's all till your friend here rang the bell this morning at ten o'clock."

Krasno said, "Well, keep right on sweating them. Hell, there's no *evidence* which of 'em did it. Unless we can trip one of them up on something, we're against a blank wall."

"You're darn tootin' it's a blank wall. We can't jail all of them." He turned and glowered at Mr. Smith, who was industriously polishing his gold-rimmed pince-nez glasses. Mr. Smith smiled blandly back at him.

"By the way, Lieutenant," said Mr. Smith. "Are you insured?"

"Huh?"

"Do you carry life insurance? We have a special policy for policemen and detectives. Captain Krasno here carries five thousand dollars' worth of it. He will tell you—"

"He will tell you," cut in Krasno, "to get back to the mines and keep on questioning those people. This is one of those cases that's got to be cracked while it's hot or we won't crack it at all."

"Sure, Cap," Brady turned to go.

"And be sure," said Mr. Smith, "that you ask them the right questions."

Brady got to the door, then paused to look back at Mr. Smith. "Huh?" he said.

"I told you to be sure," said Mr. Smith, "to ask them the right questions."

Brady scowled. "Maybe you could. Maybe you know who done it?"

"Possibly I do." Mr. Smith replaced the well-polished glasses and regarded Brady through them. Brady looked at Krasno and then back at Mr. Smith.

"Well," he said, "what should I ask them?"

Mr. Smith smiled again. "I fear, Lieutenant, that the particular questions I have in mind could be asked only by me."

"You mean," Brady was breathing a little hard, "that you know, or think you know, who done those murders?"

Mr. Smith nodded brightly. "I know or think I know. You put it very well, Lieutenant."

"And you know why he started to tie up what's-his-name—Larkin—and didn't finish the job?"

"I am reasonably certain. But first I would wish to speak to the three suspects separately. Perhaps about fifteen minutes with each, possibly a little longer than that."

Brady looked at Krasno. Almost defensively he said, "Can you vouch for this guy, Cap? You know him and I don't. But he's got an idea anyway and damned if I have."

Krasno cleared his throat. He said, "Well, yeah, he's all right, but—" He turned to the dapper little insurance agent. "Listen, Mr. Smith, we can't let you talk to them privately. If I'm present, it will be all right."

Mr. Smith shook his head sadly. "I'm afraid it would defeat my purpose, Captain. Well, you said you had no further need of my presence, so I'll—uh—take my leave. Good-by."

He was almost to the door when Krasno's "Hey!" made him turn.

Krasno was scowling, but he said, "All right, you win."

"Thank you," said Mr. Smith. "Where can I find the—ah—suspects?"

"Upstairs, in the two bedrooms on the north side. The Standishes are both in their room, but if you want to talk to them separately—"

"Thank you," Mr. Smith interrupted, "but it will not be necessary. Probably it is better that I see both of them at once."

Mr. Smith started briskly up the stairs.

And forty minutes later, by Krasno's watch, he came briskly down them. He beamed at Krasno and Brady. "The interviews were highly successful," he said. "And now, what do you wish to know?"

"Whattya think we want to know?" Brady demanded. "Who killed Gaby and Larkin?"

"Oh, that," said Mr. Smith. "I thought possibly you'd see the answer by now. It's the only and obvious one. The guilty party was Mr. Larkin."

"Huh? You're cuckoo. Sure he could've killed his boss, but are you trying to tell me he committed suicide afterward?"

"Not at all," said Mr. Smith. "He killed himself, yes, but he did not commit suicide. First he poisoned Mr. Gaby—"

"Why?"

"For five thousand reasons, I imagine, Lieutenant. He was down in the will for that amount and Mr. Gaby was about to make a change in that will. I think it quite possible that he had given notice to Larkin. Probably Mr. Larkin knew of that bequest and realized he was going to lose it. And this week end there was an unusual situation—three guests in the house, all heirs, and—"

"But how'd he kill himself?"

"All heirs," repeated Mr. Smith, "and all due to be suspected if Mr. Gaby was killed. And Larkin would be found bound and gagged in the closet. His story would be that he had been getting ready to take Mr. Gaby's nightcap of whiskey to him and someone had seized him from behind and overpowered him—which would have been easy as he was a very small man and quite elderly. It would have been very difficult to disprove, even if you'd doubted the story."

"You mean," Brady said, "that he waited till the others had gone to bed and then mixed the prussic acid with the whiskey, took it to Gaby, and then came out here to tie himself up in the closet?"

"Yes. If he'd been found there, the presumption would be that one of the heirs had done it, then taken the whiskey in to Gaby with some story of having come down to the kitchen for something."

"That makes sense, but—but what happened?"

Mr. Smith smiled patiently. "He sat down in the closet and tied his ankles. Undoubtedly he'd practiced some way of tying his own wrists—there are many ways of doing a pretty convincing job of that, I understand—but before tying them, he'd have to put on the gag. He did that and then lost interest and never finished."

"Why?"

"He died," said Mr. Smith. "Remember that big stain on the sink where he'd spilled some of the whisky-and-prussic acid in mixing them? Naturally, he'd wiped that up with the dishrag right away. And when, after delivering the decanter, he came back to tie himself up—well, that dishrag was what anybody else would have used as a gag. He forgot that it was soaked with prussic acid and used it.

"He was not an experienced criminal, of course, and he would have been highly excited and scared just at that moment and not thinking as clearly as he would have been at another—"

Brady whistled. "Cap!" he said, "that's it. The little guy's right. The only way it could have happened. It makes sense."

Krasno took a deep breath. "I'll be damned," he said. "Staring us in the face all the time and we didn't— Say, when did you guess the answer?"

"As soon, Captain, as you remarked how strange it was that someone had started to tie up Larkin and not finished the job and I started wondering about whether he'd got the poison before or after the gag had been applied. You said it didn't make sense either way and you were quite right. But if he got the prussic acid neither before nor after he put on that gag—"

"The hell," said Brady. And then, as a cloud drifts across the sun, bewilderment settled on his face. "But what did questioning the Standishes and this Lee guy have to do with it? What could you find out from them that would prove it?"

"Nothing, Lieutenant," said Mr. Smith "Nothing at all. I didn't talk to them about the murder. You will recall that I did not say that that was what I wanted to see them about."

"Well, yeah, I guess so, but dammit, what did—"

"People who have just seen sudden death," said Mr. Smith calmly, "are excellent prospects for life insurance. So are people who have just inherited large sums of money. The Standishes and Mr. Lee, therefore, were perfect prospects. Talking to them here, alone and in privacy, gave me the inside track. I sold forty thousand dollars worth of insurance just now, gentlemen, and I thank you for the opportunity. Good afternoon."

Brady closed his eyes tightly and listened to Mr. Smith's brisk footsteps reach the front door. He heard the door open and close, then slowly he opened his eyes again. Deliberately, he took off his hat and stared at it.

"Well," he said, "I need a new one anyway, don't I?"

And he threw it on the floor and stamped on it.